# Acclaim For the
# MAX ALLA

"Crime fiction aficionados are in for a treat...a neo-pulp noir classic."

—*Chicago Tribune*

"No one can twist you through a maze with as much intensity and suspense as Max Allan Collins."

—*Clive Cussler*

"Collins never misses a beat...All the stand-up pleasures of dime-store pulp with a beguiling level of complexity."

— *Booklist*

"Collins has an outwardly artless style that conceals a great deal of art."

—*New York Times Book Review*

"Max Allan Collins is the closest thing we have to a 21st-century Mickey Spillane and...will please any fan of old-school, hardboiled crime fiction."

—*This Week*

"A suspenseful, wild night's ride [from] one of the finest writers of crime fiction that the U.S. has produced."

—*Book Reporter*

"This book is about as perfect a page turner as you'll find."

—*Library Journal*

"Bristling with suspense and sexuality, this book is a welcome addition to the Hard Case Crime library."

—*Publishers Weekly*

"A total delight…fast, surprising, and well-told."
—*Deadly Pleasures*

"Strong and compelling reading."
—*Ellery Queen's Mystery Magazine*

"Max Allan Collins [is] like no other writer."
—*Andrew Vachss*

"Collins breaks out a really good one, knocking over the hard-boiled competition (Parker and Leonard for sure, maybe even Puzo) with a one-two punch: a feisty storyline told bittersweet and wry…nice and taut…the book is unputdownable. Never done better."
—*Kirkus Reviews*

"Rippling with brutal violence and surprising sexuality...I savored every turn."
—*Bookgasm*

"Masterful."
—*Jeffery Deaver*

"Collins has a gift for creating low-life believable characters …a sharply focused action story that keeps the reader guessing till the slam-bang ending. A consummate thriller from one of the new masters of the genre."
—*Atlanta Journal Constitution*

"For fans of the hardboiled crime novel…this is powerful and highly enjoyable reading, fast moving and very, very tough."
—*Cleveland Plain Dealer*

"Entertaining…full of colorful characters…a stirring conclusion."
—*Detroit Free Press*

“Collins makes it sound as though it really happened.”
—*New York Daily News*

“An exceptional storyteller.”
—*San Diego Union Tribune*

“Nobody does it better than Max Allan Collins.”
—*John Lutz*

*He was aiming my own nine-millimeter automatic at me. The extra ammo clip he had confiscated and tucked away somewhere. He was out of his topcoat and wearing a black track suit with white stripes down the sleeves and legs. If he was here to force me into dressing like that, he'd have to shoot me.*

*I'd fallen asleep in the clothes I'd worn since yesterday and through the night, jeans and a long-sleeve navy t-shirt. I'd like to tell you I had a throwing knife or small revolver tucked at the small of my back, but I didn't.*

*The only thing I had going for me was that I was alive. That he hadn't killed me while I slept, which is what I deserved; but I'd only been awake maybe two seconds before I realized he was here for more than fulfilling a contract.*

*"Wondering why you're still alive?" he asked. He had a baritone voice that would have gone well with a gig as a late-night jazz-spinning disc jockey. Soothing, almost, except for the part where he was a hired killer holding my own gun on me.*

*"I am," I admitted. "Pleasantly so."*

*"Thing is," he said, "I know who you are…"*

**HARD CASE CRIME BOOKS**
**BY MAX ALLAN COLLINS:**

QUARRY
QUARRY'S LIST
QUARRY'S DEAL
QUARRY'S CUT
QUARRY'S VOTE
THE LAST QUARRY
THE FIRST QUARRY
QUARRY IN THE MIDDLE
QUARRY'S EX
THE WRONG QUARRY
QUARRY'S CHOICE
QUARRY IN THE BLACK
QUARRY'S CLIMAX
QUARRY'S WAR *(graphic novel)*
KILLING QUARRY

DEADLY BELOVED
SEDUCTION OF THE INNOCENT
TWO FOR THE MONEY

DEAD STREET *(with Mickey Spillane)*
THE CONSUMMATA *(with Mickey Spillane)*

# Killing QUARRY

by **Max Allan Collins**

**A HARD CASE CRIME BOOK**
(HCC-142)
*First Hard Case Crime edition: November 2019*

Published by
Titan Books
A division of Titan Publishing Group Ltd
144 Southwark Street
London SE1 0UP
in collaboration with Winterfall LLC



Print edition ISBN 978-1-78565-945-4
E-book ISBN 978-1-78909-033-8

Design direction by Max Phillips
*www.signalfoundry.com*

Typeset by Swordsmith Productions



Printed in the United States of America

*Visit us on the web at www.HardCaseCrime.com*

*In memory of*
*BILL CRIDER*
*(1941–2018)*
*Writer, friend,*
*excellent at both.*

*"After the war, they took Army dogs*
*and rehabilitated them for civilian life.*
*But they turned soldiers into civilians immediately,*
*and let 'em sink or swim."*
AUDIE MURPHY

## AUTHOR'S NOTE

For various reasons, the Quarry novels have jumped around in time, sometimes taking place during the protagonist's "hitman" years of the early to mid-1970s, others dealing with the later '70s and '80s and even occasionally thereafter.

Readers concerned about chronology may find it useful to know that *Killing Quarry* takes place a year or so before *Quarry's Vote* (aka *Primary Target*).

M.A.C.

# KILLING QUARRY

# ONE

When you get to the point of losing track of how many people you've killed, you might want to take a moment and reevaluate.

That's where my head was at, on the drive from my A-frame in Wisconsin on Paradise Lake to Naperville, Illinois, where someone I didn't know stood a good chance of being on the wrong end of my nine-millimeter Browning automatic.

But if I said I felt compelled to stop using murder as a tool of my trade, I would be lying. And guilt or remorse had nothing to do with it, either. It was everything else that went with my work that was bringing me down—the business shit, like explaining to somebody they've been targeted for death. And the boring parts, like when the background gets laid in, in a book.

For example, do I really have to tell you any more about myself besides I did two tours in Vietnam? Maybe that I was a Marine sniper would help. Or that Reagan was in his second term as president when the things I'm about to share happened. That should do it, right? From that, you can guesstimate how old I was when all this went down, and around what year it did. Even I can do that math.

What else.

I was five ten, one-hundred-seventy pounds, light brown hair, dark brown eyes. Or maybe dark brown hair and dark blue eyes. Telling you exactly what I looked like would be like sharing my real name with you, which I'm not about to. I was just a guy in a restaurant at the next table or on the bar stool beside you; a glance and a smile and a nod. Pleasant-looking, boyish, fuck-able, at Last Call anyway (ladies only, please).

Leave it at that.

Not enough? Well, usually I went by Jack Something. Not always. Think of me as Quarry, which is what the Broker called me.

Broker had these supposedly clever code-type names for his entire stable of contract killers—I was Quarry, "empty and carved out of rock." My partner, dead by the time this takes place, was "Boyd"—a gay guy who "boyed." Get it? The Broker's dead, too, and maybe you already figured out who made that happen.

Or maybe you've read one or more of the memoirs of mine that preceded this one, in which case I'm fine with you skimming a while. For those who haven't....

After I came home from the Nam (yes, we put "the" in front of it, don't ask me why) and killed my wife's boyfriend, I attracted some attention in the papers. Not nationwide—southern California, near San Diego where I'd done my basic training and met the girl. Anyway, I had medals and they decided not to prosecute. I was arraigned, but that's as far as it went.

Somehow the Broker found out about me. There had been outraged editorials when I was arrested, and outraged editorials when they cut me loose. Maybe some of that got picked up by a wire service. Maybe Broker had a clipping service. He must have had some kind of feelers out, for soldiers prone to not fitting back in.

He was a country club type, prematurely white hair with a skimpy matching mustache, slender and handsome in an executive kind of way, well-dressed but not flashy. Leisure suits, mostly. He asked me if I wanted to kill people for good money, having killed plenty for chump change.

I was interested.

For five years or so, I carried out contracts with a partner, the one whose corny code-name was Boyd. Broker's method was to have one of us go in to a location a few weeks or so early to research the target, get the pattern down, look for…windows of opportunity. This was done by the passive half of the duo. The active half would roll in a few days before the hit was set to go down, the passive partner filling in his active half, there to do the deed.

I much preferred active, and that was fine with Boyd, who liked the passive role. A catcher at heart, not a pitcher. But at the Broker's insistence, we switched it up now and then. Sometimes it was my turn to be on the bottom. Just to keep our skills honed.

Anyway, I was Broker's fair-haired boy until I wasn't, and he double-crossed me. So pretty soon he was dead and I came to have his list. What list, you ask? Well, today they would call it a database, but this was definitely analog days. Not even analog—we're talking pen-and-ink or typewriter.

The list had the names and addresses and fairly detailed info on everybody in the Broker's stable, including photos. I put it that way before, stable, like we were all sharing a barn or something. Really, other than the handful of others we worked with, none of us knew each other.

That meant the list's fifty-plus hitmen, to use the TV term, were mostly unknown to me. Again, except for any potential partners I'd been put with early on, the Broker looking for a good fit. Once he was satisfied with the mix, the Broker liked to keep a team together over the long haul.

So unless you didn't get along with who you'd been assigned—or that partner got killed and needed replacing—you knew jack shit about the others in that "stable" of Broker's. Just thumbing through the list, mostly men and a handful of females, I saw almost exclusively former military. Vietnam was a terrific breeding ground for psychos and sociopaths. How I managed to come out of there as grounded as I did, I'll never know.

Earlier, just trying to get your attention, I mentioned having to explain to somebody that he or she had been targeted for death. But you may have taken that wrong. Actually, I kind of meant for you to.

When I was carrying out contracts, I never explained to the marks why they were about to die. Instead, I tried to make it as quick and painless as possible, for both of us. Only a psycho would have done otherwise. I took no pleasure in killing. Pride, yes, as a professional. But, really, not a whole lot of that, either.

For me, killing was just a living.

How explaining to a guy that he's been marked for death comes into it is this: the list. I figured there must be some way to use that list to my benefit, to take advantage of what these days they call a skill set.

But I had no desire to use the names to become the new Broker. Just didn't suit me, booking gigs for guys with guns, playing daddy to a bunch of damaged goods. Wasn't long, though, before I came up with a plan.

You know the kind—like in the movies or on the tube (Christ, that dates me), when somebody says, "This is so crazy, it just might work!"

And it did work.

I would pick a name in the murder business from the Broker's list, go to wherever that subject was living his fake life, and set up surveillance. Which was the worst part, admittedly. Because suddenly I was in the passive role.

Which sometimes required great patience—people in the murder business don't work steady, after all. You don't punch a clock, you punch the mark. Me, I used to do maybe four or five jobs a year. Tops.

So in my new role, surveillance could last a fuck of an open-ended long time.

But eventually my subject would lead me to the mark. This

would require some detective work on my part. For example, what if I'd followed somebody whose role was the passive one?

*Shit!*

More surveillance!

More often, though, I'd drawn the active half. That was partly luck, but also the list sometimes specified a preference. Active would check in with passive, and you didn't have to be Sherlock Holmes to get a fix on who was being staked out and targeted.

That's where having people skills comes in handy.

I would approach the target. Yes, you're ahead of me. This is indeed where I would explain to somebody that he or she had been marked for murder. How I did this varied from sticking a gun in a guy's ribs to just cornering him in a public place.

Sorry about putting you through all this boring background. I wish I could tell you that skipping it is fine, but you rookies better not. Some basics are coming.

Let's start with why somebody who grew up in Ohio (if it *was* Ohio) in a quietly middle-class neighborhood (that much is true) turned into a killer for hire. Obviously, Vietnam played a role. And coming home to find my wife in bed fucking another guy probably should be factored in, too.

Now I'm repeating myself, but I never claimed to be a writer, and anyway the point is—Uncle Sugar developed in me certain skills. Skill set, remember? I learned about firearms, and as a sniper, I learned to kill without compassion and at a distance. That "at a distance" idea is both literal and figurative.

What the Broker explained to me, when he recruited my services, was that people who have been selected for murder usually have it coming. That's glib, I realize; but there's often truth in it—the marks have stolen from employers or cheated on spouses or diddled business partners, or otherwise put themselves in the position of the world around them being better off without them in it.

They may even have killed people themselves, got away with it, and now *really* have it coming.

Circumstances have dictated that, due to the illegal nature of a mob-tied business, say, going to the cops isn't a good option. Or consulting a divorce lawyer isn't either, because a pre-nup or religion or some stupid damn thing gets in the way.

Which means not every victim deserves it, no matter what the Broker said. Not everybody in the crosshairs put themselves there by their own wayward actions. That's just a recruiter's trick, like telling you you're making the world safe for democracy when some poor little yellow (not in the cowardly way) bastard is just trying to keep invaders off his pathetic little piece of rice paddy.

Plenty of people get quietly killed because their favorite uncle left his fortune to his favorite niece, and the nephew nobody liked, especially the uncle, has another idea. Some young wives have old husbands who stubbornly refuse to die of natural causes, and the death of said spouse is preferable to divorce. And some crooked businessmen have honest partners who just get to be a pain in the ass.

Yet even if they don't deserve it, any mark has managed to come between someone and what that someone wants...enough so for that someone to hire the mark's fucking death. And that is a decision made a long time before an asshole like me came along with a way to make that happen.

Such a death has already been decided. Once the down payment has been made, the intended target is just an obituary walking around, waiting to go to press. You don't have to have big money to hire somebody dead. Fifty bucks in the right dive can swing it.

But if you wind up giving money to a middleman like the Broker, you've got coin all right. You're rich or close to it. And specialty murders, like accidents or frame-ups, are on the menu. Not my specialty, though. In that rarefied climate, I was neither fine dining nor fast food—more like an old-fashioned steak house. Nothing fancy. Just a bullet in a steer's brain. And, in the case of a "suicide," a baked potato with all the trimmings on the side.

Now I know I referred to this as "the murder business," but it isn't really. That's just words. Me? I was no more a murderer than a gun or a bullet is. Firearms and ammunition and yours truly, we're just about the mechanics of the matter.

You see, murder is personal, like when I kicked the jack out and crushed my wife's lover under that little sportscar. Killing, however, is a fait accompli, as the French said when they left Vietnam.

So if you're thinking I was some kind of contract-killing Robin Hood, exorcizing my guilt and remorse by warning the potential victims of other contract killers, well, think again. I was a businessman charging for a service. Like a lube job or fries with that. As for informing the victim that death was coming for him, that was complimentary.

Like the drug dealers say, first one's free....

But taking out the contract killers—preventing the immediate threat to somebody's ability to breathe—that'll cost you. And it costs you more if I can determine—and remove—who took the contract out on you.

I had been doing that for almost ten years—quite successfully—when I picked a name off the Broker's list and set out for Naperville to try to save another life.

I'm just that kind of guy.

# TWO

Winter was almost over, but it was still cold.

Spring wouldn't show up for a while yet and the skeletal trees with their bony branches seemed to scream autumn till you noticed the occasional clumps of snow stubbornly clinging. The ground had some snow, too, plopped here and there like oversize bird droppings.

Going from the Lake Geneva vicinity, barely inside Wisconsin's border, to Naperville in the greater Chicago area made for one of my easier trips to a name and location plucked from the Broker's list. We're talking maybe an hour and forty minutes, depending on traffic, after white-patchy farmland turned into urban sprawl.

The dark-blue, mildly battered Chevy Impala, a decade old, had decent heat, a radio-cassette player and surprising pick-up. This was hardly competition for my Batman-black Firebird at home, but I'd felt lucky to pick it up for under a grand in Muskego, where I would sell it back on my return. The used car lot, where I'd done business before, even let me store the Firebird in back at a pittance of a weekly rate.

I never used my own car on a job.

The wind rattled the windows and nuts and bolts that weren't exactly new-car-lot fresh, but my fleece-lined bomber jacket did right by me, and I left my leather driving gloves on. The latter were nicely snug for use with my nine-millimeter Browning, which was on the seat next to me, under a spread-open *Playboy*. I took Highway 12 all the way, some of it four-lane, some two-lane, but a direct route. I had some homemade cassettes along—

Beach Boys; Beatles, for memories; Bangles and Blondie, to convince myself I wasn't an old man yet.

Naperville, thirty miles or so outside of Chicago, was booming, like so many other suburbs in an area whose populations had swelled up when the East-West Tollway went in. Right now I was on Ogden Avenue, clogged in traffic in a commercial garden blossoming with AllState, Kwik-Kopy and Burger King signs. I pulled in for a sub sandwich at the Original Italian U-Boat (slogan: *Accept No Sub-stitutes!*) and asked for directions to Ridgeview Lane.

Which proved to be a typical suburban Pleasant Valley Sunday kind of street, two quiet blocks in a subdivision called Steeple Run. We're talking plenty of trees currently growing nothing but snowy daubs on otherwise bare branches, and butch-haircut lawns of brown and green and white, no color dominating. Not that this was a cookie-cutter area—each house was distinctive, in its non-distinctive way, a ranch-style here, a split-level there, plenty of two-stories.

But a sleepy, prosperous neighborhood like this did me no favors.

This was a street—a narrow two-lane street at that—where everybody knew their neighbors. By name. Kids included. Hell, they probably knew each other's car—fuck, license plate. Somebody right now could be calling the Steeple Run Homeowners Association rep or even the Naperville police to sound the alarm that some unknown party was driving a 1970s-era relic through the area.

The house in question was painfully cheerful, like maybe the Partridge Family lived here—two modern canary-yellow stories trimmed blue with a peaked two-car attached garage. In the driveway was a Cadillac DeVille, recent vintage, pale yellow with a white Cabriolet-style vinyl half-roof. Color-coordinated, yet. If his next Caddy was green, would the house get a paint job?

Surveillance difficulties abounded. Houses here were fairly close together, the lawns shallow along the narrow concrete ribbon of Ridgeview Lane. Driveways were for parking, curbs strictly decorative. Park your wheels on one side of the street and you'd be in the opposite homeowner's face.

At the same time, sidewalks and for that matter front yards were free of toys or skates or bikes or any other signs of life except for the nice new (or at least new-ish) cars in the drives of two-car garages. The only other indications of inhabitants were the garbage cans set out for tomorrow's pick-up.

Maybe I could get a job as a garbage man—that would allow me to unobtrusively stake out the house on Ridgeview Lane for as much as a once-a-week minute. No, *better* than a minute! I could probably get five or even ten minutes out of my efforts, if I could master the motor skills needed to empty cans in back of the truck while keeping my eye on this particular house....

Or, with my background in the service of my country, possibly I could land a gig at the post office as a mail carrier and secretly keep watch on the neighborhood six days a week, an hour or so a day. This assumed I could pass the civil service exam, and didn't shoot any dogs trying to bite me. Hey! What about a paper route?

At this point, by the way, I was on my third slow pass through the two blocks of Ridgeview Lane, and about at the end of what I dared do around here for now.

Yet, childish sarcasm aside, one possibility did wink dangerously at my desperate needs, like jailbait behind the Naperville Mall corndog counter. A house across the way—not *directly* across the way, but two houses down—had a big FOR SALE sign in the lawn.

I almost didn't bother. I almost bailed anyway. Already I was getting disheartened about what I'd been doing these past ten or so years, and if you factored in the five or six years with the Broker, and the two tours in Nam (sometimes we *don't* use the "the"), I mean, who needed this?

Didn't I have money in the bank? In a number of banks actually? I'd scored well this past decade, while living modestly; and I'd had a number of unexpected windfalls over the years. Now and then you stumble into money when you take down evil pricks. Really, why not seriously consider retirement?

Maybe to a house on Ridgeview Lane.

Which gave me a couple of reasons to check out that house across the way, two doors down, where I pulled into the empty drive and moved the nine millimeter from under the *Playboy* and into my waistband, under the zipped bomber jacket.

Then I got out and went over to stand on the edge of the drive, hands on hips, gawking at the house in prospective buyer mode. The slant of the lawn and glint of the sun didn't allow for an easy look in the windows. Best play it safe. Sort of safe.

I walked up to the faux-rustic two-story and rang the bell. I could hear it sound faintly within. My hunch was no one was home—no car in the drive, no sign of activity. But somebody might answer, and if they did, I would inquire about seeing the house.

Presumably whoever answered, depending on how hungry they were to sell, would give me an impromptu walk-through, or remind me that the realtor's name and phone number were on the yard sign.

Anyway, none of that mattered, because three tries on the bell went unanswered. By now someone—possibly any number of someones, including the person I was there to stake out (and possibly family members of his) could well be watching. Wouldn't they be, in this kind of neighborhood?

So I did not try the door. That would be rude. Might seem suspicious. Could even be gauche, if I knew what that meant exactly.

What I did instead was more in keeping with what any innocent person interested in possibly buying the house might do—I got on my toes and peeked in a few windows. And the news was good.

No furniture.

So maybe I was still in business after all. Having no homeowner to deal with meant I had options. For example, I could go to the realtor with fake I.D. (which of course I carried) and begin negotiations to buy, doing my best not to put much, or any, money down. Just do what it took to tie a ribbon around the property.

Or, better, I could come in after dark and slip into the place and play squatter. With luck, the water would be on, which meant drinking water and toilet privileges. Maybe some of the appliances had been left in the house. I already had some stuff in the trunk of the Impala for just such a contingency—a little portable TV, space heater, an inflatable camping mattress, pillow from home, portable radio, plastic ice chest.

I would find a grocery store to buy bags of ice, sandwich makings, and six-packs of Diet Coke. I don't drink beer on the job. Don't drink it much ever, actually. Very clean-cut type. Add no facial hair to your mental image.

This camping-out approach I had used in the Broker days when the passive role came my way. And in recent years, I'd occasionally gone this route, too. This was not the first time I'd consigned myself to a mid-range rung of suburban Hell.

Walking around outside the house, I found a cement patio with a covered barbecue grill and not much else. Edging up to snow-touched shrubbery, I checked more windows, but also looked for access, in terms of both the house itself (basement windows—nice) and behind the place, which was heavily wooded.

Good.

I could sneak in that way easy enough, after dark. With luck, I could get inside, check the place out, determining the best window onto the street with a view on the house across the way, two doors down.

Then I'd look the garage over, probably find it empty, and locate the garage door opener, likely just inside the door connecting to the house. Sometime deep into the night, I could move my car into the garage, empty the trunk of my accessories, and play Campfire Girl in a stranger's domain. I had everything but marshmallows and a stick.

I would also have to make arrangements for quickly disassembling my surveillance perch, and find somewhere close to stow the gear (again, quickly), should a car or two pull up for a realtor showing of the house to prospective buyers. That was a routine I'd been through many times, back in Broker days, and about as fun as a surprise inspection in a barracks.

But nobody said life was going to be easy.

"Can I help you?"

The voice was male, friendly and mildly threatening.

He was in the back yard of the house next door—to my left as I faced the rear of my would-be squatter's paradise. A big guy, fleshy, in a gray overcoat and matching face. Kind of a junior-high football coach type. Probably the assistant coach, who worked with the line.

I grinned and strode over to him, extended a hand. "Jack Matthews," I said.

"Carl Burgis," he said, half-smiling, the other half of his face skeptical. He had light-color thinning hair and a wide oval of a face. Maybe forty. Lots of lines, but then he was partly frowning, so....

"I'm not generally a window peeker," I said with a laugh, hands in my bomber jacket pockets, rocking on my Reeboks. "I just saw the 'for sale' sign, stopped, and knocked and…nobody home." I shrugged. "So I thought I'd take a look-see."

"No harm done," he said, like maybe there had been. Under the topcoat was a t-shirt. He'd seen me out a window and threw the coat on and came out to check on me.

With a nod toward the rustic two-story, I said, "You don't happen to know how much they're asking?"

He grunted a laugh. First sign he was warming. "*Too* much."

"How much is too much?"

"Hundred and fifty K. Been sitting for months. They moved to California. Maybe they like having two house payments. I sure wouldn't."

"Me neither! What do houses go for around here, generally?"

"Round a hundred. I paid eighty, but that was five years ago. What do you for a living, son?"

Tiny bit skeptical still, but pretty warm now.

I said, "I'm a teacher, but so is my wife, so we have two incomes. I think we could make it here."

"I'm a teacher myself," he said, grinning. "And so is *my* wife. I'm a coach. Football."

Am I good?

Hands on his hips now. "Where are you teaching, son?"

"You familiar with St. Charles?"

"Yeah, of course. Nice little town. Don't really know anybody up that way, though. Not in our conference."

I was glad of that, because that meant I didn't have to pull any other names of Illinois towns out of my ass.

"Well," I said, "St. Charles is where I'm teaching. English. Assistant swimming coach, too."

"Very good."

We chatted a while, about how long my commute would be—half an hour to forty-five minutes—and other small talk. His wife was a history teacher. And so on. That he'd seen me was a bit of a problem, but not enough to make me change my plans. He was a nice guy. I hoped I wouldn't have to kill him.

With that my only misgiving, I walked around to the front where my car was parked in the drive. My hand was on the key in the ignition when someone came out of the house across the way. Down two doors.

The name he used here was Bruce Simmons. He was about my age, my size, similar build, but with dark hair longer than mine, kept neatly in place by what people insist on calling "product." His eyes were dark, too, his face narrow but handsome, nose and chin pointed but not in an aggressive way. Tan, either sunning bed or vacation. He wore a gray topcoat but it only came to mid-thigh and under it was a black turtleneck. Maybe a gun, too. Maybe not.

But for sure he carried a good-size brown canvas travel bag.

This he stowed in the back seat, and as he did, a woman in her late twenties or early thirties came out—not dressed for the weather, just to say goodbye—with a cute little boy of maybe four tagging along at her side, tugging on her nearest sleeve.

She was a looker. Her hair was big and black and frizzy, and her nice slim body was in a denim pantsuit. Her face was pale and her mouth was wide and red with lipstick, white with teeth. The little kid, also with frizzy black hair, was wearing—hell, I don't remember. Whatever little kids wear. He was cute. Leave it at that.

Anyway, Simmons had apparently forgotten his shaving kit, because she brought it out to him. He took it and smiled at her and they kissed. Nothing too elaborate—what would the

Homeowner's Association say? But it was warm and real. The kid was dancing, his eyes on daddy.

Who picked him up and gave him a kiss on the forehead and put him back down.

He got in the Caddy, tossing the shaving kit in the backseat with the canvas bag, and started the engine and waved at them over its throaty purr and backed out. They waved at him like he was the *Titanic* pulling away from the dock, and in a way, wasn't he?

Because it was very likely I'd be killing him, and if you think I'm terrible for that—and I'm not saying I'm not—but if you're feeling sorry for his little family, think about it. How many families had *he* ruined? For a living? How much better off would they be, without him but with whatever funds he'd stashed away for them?

She could do better. With him gone, nobody would come kidnap that little boy to get at daddy. Or rape and kill the looker mommy in denim in revenge for something daddy did. Daddy was a killer. Don't feel sorry for him. If you're smart, you won't feel sorry for me, either.

I didn't wait long to pull out of the drive and fall in behind him. Didn't stay that way long, though—plenty of traffic even at off times in that part of the world, to make it simple enough to keep a couple or three cars between me and him.

He headed north. It was the tail end of rush hour and he took the tollway to Skokie, where he gave money to a cigar-smoking loud-jacketed used car salesman, leaving the guy the Caddy in exchange for a fake-woody Mercury station wagon, half a decade old. Great minds think alike, although I had to admit I hadn't thought about ever picking up a station wagon. For a big vehicle, they didn't come less suspicious.

And if you had to move a body, wow. Good choice.

He ate at Skokie, too—a deli diner, a mom-and-pop joint called Jack's. I ate there myself, the place big enough for me to maintain a distance (Simmons in a booth, me at the counter) but still keep an eye on him. We both had the Reuben. This was a Jewish enclave, Skokie, and they knew their way around corned beef.

My distant dining companion did not seem to be looking around, surreptitiously or otherwise. He was just a guy having a sandwich with fries (hand-cut, very good). And why should he? He had no reason for care, beyond switching cars. He wasn't on the job, he was on his way *to* a job. Why would anybody be following him?

Which did make my task somewhat easier.

But when he cut over to Highway 12, still heading north, darkness settling in, I began to have misgivings. If he was on his way to my part of the world for a gig, I couldn't have any part of it. Too damn risky. Already this thing had started feeling risky—once the traffic thinned, past the Chicago area, keeping distance between my car and his while not losing him was no easy fucking task.

Then we were in Wisconsin. The Lake Geneva area isn't very far over the border, maybe twelve miles. As we headed that way, still on Highway 12, I knew I would have to bail unless he kept on going north, maybe to Fond Du Lac or Oshkosh or Green Bay. Maybe some popular Packer got a contract taken out on him by some sore loser Bears fan.

But my man didn't keep going north. He took a turn and then so did this whole goddamn mess. His turn took him through very familiar lanes lined with trees, many of them evergreen and holding onto the snow, and then he pulled into the parking lot of a rambling two-story establishment, open in off-season to serve the sparse population of locals.

Wilma's Welcome Inn was a combination gas station, restaurant, grocery store and lodge, which was even shabbier now that it was run by the late Wilma's husband Charley. Nothing terribly significant about this oddball establishment, except perhaps for one thing.

You could see my A-frame from there.

## THREE

The family man named Simmons from Ridgeview Lane in Naperville, Illinois, was clearly on my Paradise Lake turf now. What that meant wasn't exactly clear, as the Buffalo Springfield song said, but pretty damn clear nonetheless, and while Wilma's Welcome Inn had a good reputation for killer comfort food, I doubted this prick drove all the way to Wisconsin for the chili. He'd already eaten, after all.

A few parking places—several filled by locals—hugged the face of the building, but this time of year the front entry and the dining room were shuttered. Alongside the Inn, at the right, wooden steps led up to a little landing, bordering a drive back to an expansive parking lot sloping to some trees that did not block an excellent view of my cottage on the lake. Not a single car in that rear lot, either, to obstruct.

Another interesting fun fact: I owned Wilma's Welcome Inn. Curiouser and curiouser, as Lewis Carroll said. Or was it Walt Disney?

Back around when I'd first started utilizing the Broker's list for fun and profit, a guy who I'd worked with in the early Broker days, called Turner, just happened to show up on my turf like this. In that instance, it proved to be a coincidence, but I'd had to treat it like it probably wasn't and some of the ramifications were…unfortunate.

Starting with Wilma of Welcome Inn fame. She was a big fat gal, one of those Mama Cass-type women who didn't have to work hard to fill out a muumuu. But she was pretty and funny and really did make the best damn chili in Wisconsin. People in the off-season sometimes actually did drive up here for the comfort food. Beer-batter walleye, too, and barbecue ribs.

Probably not Simmons, though.

Anyway, Wilma. We would kid each other, and flirt, and I'd say tasteless things, like, "If you wanna go upstairs, honey, that's cool—but we'll have to hump twice, for me to break even."

And she and her chins would jiggle with laughter, and the funny thing was I did kind of dig her. But she wound up getting killed, in the Turner fuck-up. So did Turner.

Her common-law hubby was a grizzled bald bartender named Charley who looked like a shaved Shar Pei, and he and Wilma's teenage niece wound up owning the place. When the girl got to legal age, she sold out to me and so did Charley, who was better at drawing beers than keeping books. The Welcome Inn gave me some income when I needed it and had its money-laundering benefits as well.

I had little to do with the place at first, but I sometimes worked in the filling station's modest garage—I'd tinkered with cars since high school—and had gradually made the ancient building less ramshackle, without losing its charm. Or mine either, for that matter. So, over the years, some remodeling got done.

I pulled in at Wilma's and took the last parking spot of the handful in the small front lot. Right next to Simmons. I sat there for a while with the motor running, both the car's and my own, studying that station wagon like it still had its driver in it. He might come right back out, if he'd just stopped for directions, and I would deal with him right here. Nobody around.

Because, let's face it, I knew what he was here for.

I was the mark.

All my list shenanigans had finally caught up with me, it

would seem, and at this point why and who and how was not my prime concern. Survival was.

My two most basic beliefs may appear contradictory: that life and death are meaningless, and survival is everything. That's a circle I've never spent much time squaring, but if I strike you as deeply philosophical, you really haven't been paying attention.

So I sat there with my bomber jacket zipper down and my Browning in my lap, attaching the noise suppressor that had been in my right-hand jacket pocket. If Simmons returned to his station wagon, having gotten his directions—which wouldn't take long, since my A-frame was in spitting distance—I'd be ready. Ready enough, anyway.

I was still operating off the notion that Simmons didn't know what I looked like. Which was as safe an assumption as any in this unsafe game. A higher risk was that the bastard might—*might*—recognize me from the Skokie diner. But he sure hadn't seemed to be scoping out that joint while he chowed down on corned beef.

Of course, he maybe could have made my car. The Chevy Impala was a fairly invisible ride, but this was a pro and he might have tagged it, despite my efforts to never be driving the car directly behind him. Traffic had been light, once Chicago was history, and maybe the Impala and I had turned up too often, in his rear-view mirror.

I hoped I wouldn't have to kill him here. *Right* here. Talk about shitting where you eat. And a silenced weapon isn't like Hollywood would have it. Think about having a bad raspy cough, how when you cover your mouth with a hand or a sleeve, it's still a cough that people can hear. But nobody was around to hear anything, at the moment, and a life was at stake.

My favorite one: mine.

An eternity of maybe three minutes passed before I slipped the nine millimeter with the noise suppressor into the right-hand bomber jacket pocket, which was plenty deep, a custom job that was almost a built-in holster, reinforced fabric too. I got out, headed around to the side entrance, went up the steps and in, through a little foyer bordered by pamphlets on racks about what a fun time was to be had around here.

The layout of Wilma's, a result of my do-it-yourself remodeling, now had a longish counter with cash register at right where you could pay for your food and check in or out of a room. During the season, two employees worked back there, sharing the register but with one handling the restaurant and the other the hotel. The rambling two-story structure's upper floor had the guest rooms. All but two room keys were hanging on the wall of little hooks, so the hotel side was not doing land-office off-season business.

Behind the register was a good-looking brunette with nice tits and a sour attitude. Her mouth had a bruised look glistening with lipstick as red as a red Corvette, half threat, half promise.

"Look what the cat drug in," she said to her employer.

Brenda had been glowing at the job interview, and we'd fucked pretty much right away—though not at the interview. What kind of boss do you take me for?

But I gradually realized *I* was the one being screwed, because she pilfered the register—not overdoing, but she did, and I never called her on it. Despite that, she liked me even less than I liked her.

She was the kind of woman who uses sex to get a job and then resents you over it—how's that for a double standard! The once a month or so that we still fucked, however, was pretty hot. Hate sex has its place. As long as it's consensual.

"That guy," I whispered to her, leaning on the counter, "where is he?"

"Why don't you speak up?" As usual she showed me a half-smirk, which was annoying and, yeah, kind of hot.

"Because I am seeking confidentiality."

She snorted a laugh and folded her arms on the impressive shelf of her white-bloused bosom, her chin back. "I thought you were out of town."

"I don't seem to be. Where's the customer?"

"He's not a local."

"I know. Where is he?"

She jerked a thumb at the wall behind her, which meant he was in the bar, which was also the restaurant this time of year. A closed dining room loomed behind me, beyond which was the convenience store/filling station, with its own register and employee. Brenda would only put up with so much.

I said, "He ask any questions?"

"Yeah."

God, I could have strangled her.

"What, Brenda, were the questions?"

"Did we have any rooms. I said, what do you think?" Half-smirk again.

"Did he take a room?"

"Yeah."

"What room, Brenda?"

"Why do you care?"

"Oh, well, maybe I think he's here to kill me."

That got something like a real laugh out of her. She of course had no idea who or what I really was. If she'd known, she might lay off the register.

"If I'd had *that* information," she said, "I woulda comped him."

"Well...it's a Chicago license plate. I was just wondering."

"Wondering what?"

"Just. Wondering."

"Confidentiality. Wondering. You have depths I never dreamed of, Jack."

"I'm an enigma wrapped up in a riddle, Brenda."

She farted with her pretty lips. "Yeah you are."

I shrugged. "I've had some interest from people in Chicago about buying us out, is all. Thought that might be what this is about."

Her frown was interested. "Buy us out? What's my piece of that?"

"A good job recommendation. Look. Don't say anything to him, Brenda. I was..."

"Wondering, right." Now she whispered, eyes narrowing, mouth curling up at each corner, taking a hand away from a breast to gesture at it. "Confidentially, I bet you're wondering when you're getting some of this sweet meat again."

"I'll let you know." Confidentially, this was the kind of girl who, when she was blowing you, you always wondered if she was about to bite it off.

As I was heading out, I asked, "Has he been up to his room yet?"

"No."

I looked at the wall of keys. "Which room? Twelve?"

"How did you know?"

"Psychic. He request that?"

"Not specifically. Said he wanted to be on that side of the building, away from traffic."

"What traffic?"

"Do I give a shit? He paid the thirty dollars."

The rooms were numbered 1 through 12, and I knew very well

that number 12 had a view on the parking lot and the A-frame cottage beyond it. For about half a second I considered going up there to wait in the room for him, but all the consequences likely to follow were just too daunting.

I was going out when she whispered again, in the nearest thing to a nice voice as she could muster for me. "I *am* a little horny, Jack."

"Good to know," I said, and went out.

What now?

If Simmons had gone upstairs, before coming down for a drink, just to stow his things, I might've been able to look through that canvas travel bag of his and determine whether he was on active or passive duty. If the latter, he would have a notebook of some kind, probably binoculars, and other gear attuned to stakeout.

And what a perfect stakeout set-up it would make. Put to shame my FOR SALE house two doors down and across the way on Ridgeview Lane back in Naperville. From Room 12 he'd have a window on my world with a restaurant, bar and gas station/ convenience store downstairs. I couldn't remember ever having it that good.

But if all I found was hardware—guns, knives, ammo, noise suppressors, what have you—that meant he was on active, and he could just walk across the parking lot and do what he came for. Wouldn't even have to move his car.

So I moved mine.

I drove home. No speed, nothing fancy. The two men here to kill me would expect their mark to live his life as usual, and I didn't want to scare them off—I wanted to invite them in…to deal with them.

And deal with them included getting whatever information I could out of the pair—and I assumed with a target like me to face down, the passive half would linger and play back-up, as was often the case anyway. I could kill one and still have another to play with.

Two bites at the apple.

A low-riding fence was between the Welcome Inn parking lot and my property, no connector. I went out the way I came in, the street in front of Wilma's almost a half-mile from the turn-off of my graveled lane, which wound back around. The night was dark, overcast, the lake a shimmering gray expanse, the trees around it silhouettes huddling like the Indians we had displaced.

I supposed there was a chance that someone was waiting for me at the cottage. So far I based everything I did on what I knew, which was the Broker's passive-active approach. No law said some other contract boys might not have their own, very different way of doing things.

So I steered with my left hand and had my riding-gloved other hand around the grip of the nine millimeter. With the noise suppressor, the weapon looked a little like a ray gun. Something modern from outer space. Only it wasn't—people had been killing with these for a long, long time.

After pulling into the crushed-rock apron and climbing out of the Impala, I went in the front way, up the few stairs to the deck, unlocking the double glass doors and slipping inside, into the big open living room. I had left my own packed bag in the trunk—might be needing to make a quick exit, after all, to someplace that was not here.

Just in case, on entering I dropped to my knees and had the nine millimeter with its extended snout out and ready. The floor was covered in a vintage shag that my knees were grateful for, but nothing else happened. I got as still as I could and listened. Only the refrigerator had anything to say.

I'd left the heat on, low but on; so it was comfy.

I slipped off the jacket, tossed it, got some lights going and opened the drapes on the glass doors, exposing the postcard view that made my property valuable. The moon had slipped out from behind the cloud cover to throw some ivory on the shimmer, but the Indians were still crowding the shores, quietly pissed.

How at once comforting and unsettling it was to be here. This place, purchased with the advance the Broker had given me when I signed on so long ago, had been my home for almost ten years. The cozy familiarity intermingled with the unsettling knowledge that a killer could see the place from his hotel room.

I gave the cottage a cautious search. Two bedrooms were at the rear, a master bedroom (which I did not use, except for dressing, but which might prompt an intruder to make the wrong assumption), a guest room (which is where I regularly slept), and a bathroom with shower.

Also toward the back was a loft with a ladder; up there I could watch TV and read—under it was the laundry room and another couple of rooms for storage and such. The big living room under the open-beamed A-frame ceiling was mostly filled by a sectional couch surrounding a black metal fireplace. Opposite was a kitchenette, behind the counter of which—post-search—I positioned myself with gun in hand.

I squatted there, poised for action or to maybe take a shit; but I didn't maintain that position long because it was wearing, and anyway this was a time of evening where I could curtail the lighting without making things look suspiciously not normal. In the loft, I put the TV on, volume down, just the tube glowing, football players knocking silently into each other.

Back down the ladder, I switched a lamp on, here and there around the place, to provide enough light for me to know exactly where any intruder might be while keeping him mostly in the dark.

I wandered a bit. Not to get used to moving around in the low light, which I could have done with my eyes closed. No, I would go to a rear window where I could keep tabs on the window that was Room 12, which right now had a light on. Of course, that didn't mean a lot—you can leave a light on in your hotel room for no better reason than it's not you paying the electric bill.

A bit later, I got out my spare binoculars from a guest room nightstand, the best pair of binocs remaining in the trunk of the Impala. Then I knelt at the sliding front doors, where I pulled back one drape a bit to be able to take a look at the houses tucked in among those trees, lining the lake.

This time of year, many—most—of those homes were vacant, shuttered for the winter. Most of the locals did not actually live on the water—those cabins (and I use cabin loosely, because many were good-size and some even lavish)—were for the tourist trade or vacation homes.

I did spot something. Not any lights on, rather a flare of reflection, thanks to the security lights outside my cabin—yes, I had a few of those, but no alarm system. I was the alarm system.

Anyway, that reflection might have been off somebody else's binoculars. And I knew just which cabin that would be. Might need to make a visit, past midnight, if I hadn't already had a visitor myself before then.

Time crawled by. I was not compulsive about checking my watch—a good fifteen minutes between glances, maybe. The light at the window of Room 12 through the trees and across the parking lot stayed on.

I glanced around at my largely darkness-shrouded surroundings. Would hate to have to leave this place. Not out of sentiment, but comfort. In a life of limited security, what I had here was pretty fucking comforting. My mind bounced between staying alert for every tiny sound and thinking about the nice, quiet life I led here. Only a few weeks a year took me away from this Fortress of Solitude, providing an influx of money and a jolt of activity.

Nearby Lake Geneva gave me access to nice restaurants, a movie multiplex and a health club, where I could swim during the winter months. Swimming is more than just exercise to me—it's a kind of zen activity, or probably would be if I for sure know what "zen" meant. I just know that swimming relaxes me—it's think or swim, a bad joke but a reality, the occasional need I had to really think something through, and the frequent times I didn't want to think at all.

For a lot of years I was a member of the Playboy Club at Geneva, a very nice lodge where I could take in some really good Vegas-style entertainment and see if I could hump more Bunnies than Hefner. I'm sure I failed at the latter, though I bet I came closer than you might think. The place closed down a few years ago, but soon came back to life as the Lake Geneva Golf and Ski Resort, a name that oddly suggested doing both at once. No Bunny costumes for the waitresses now, but plenty of bunnies just the same.

Friend of mine, Dan Clark, ran the place—one of my poker buddies for the monthly game, which always met here. At forty-something he was the oldest of the group. We had a dentist, a doctor, a video-store owner, and a seller of veterinary medicine who had to travel occasionally. That was me. A few others came in and out of the game—some were off-season, others year-round locals like yours truly.

The poker buddies were as close as I'd got to having any actual friends, other than staff at the Welcome Inn, where I was only around as needed. Odds and ends like repairs, helping out the mechanic in the little garage, banging the sour Brenda once a month or so.

I was a loner, anyway. Only child. My idea of a good time was an old movie on TV (I had a satellite dish), a paperback western to hold my interest and not tax my mind, or music dating to my high school days courtesy of my CD stereo—everything from Bobby Darin and the Beatles to the Animals and Rascals. I had an uncle who got me into Sinatra and Tony Bennett and Peggy Lee.

Just an average guy with simple tastes. I was no trouble to anybody. So who was it wanted me dead, anyway? I'd always tried not to leave any loose ends behind.

My mind wandered around like that, and that light at the Room 12 window finally winked off, around midnight.

For an hour I waited, coiled like a steel spring, nervous as a cat, and a hundred other cliches wrapped up into one big *What the fuck is going on?*

Then dawn came, and I wish that were a capital "D" dawn, a waitress at Dan Clark's Lodge who never made me wonder if she might bite my dick off when she had it in her mouth.

But no such luck. Here came the sun, as George Harrison would say in the present tense. And the sky got pink and so did the lake. Maybe in these early morning hours my prince would come. I sat up on the couch in my loft and turned off the TV, *Today Show* getting started, and thought about the warm welcome I had in mind, nine millimeter at the ready. Nobody was getting past Quarry.

Then I jerked awake.

I'd nodded off. My watch indicated I'd lost maybe an hour. An hour where I could have been snuffed or the cottage invaded.

*Shit!*

That's what I got for thinking of myself in the third person. I started over, making sure the entire place was clear. And it was. It was. Then, finally, my brain kicked in.

*What the hell, Quarry!*

*The guy just* got *to Paradise Lake. If Simmons is on surveillance, he's only getting started, and he's staying in the right room to do that. If he's here to kill me, the surveillance half of the team has been here a while, maybe in that cabin on the lake, collecting info, and Simmons has to check in with him first before making any move on me.*

I was, understandably after my long night, frazzled. I'd already gotten punchy and dropped off once. I could use some real sleep. Or at least some time to get myself centered and thinking straight.

Instead, I walked up to Wilma's Welcome Inn, cutting through the trees behind the cottage, striding across the parking lot, with my hand on the nine millimeter in my deep bomber-coat jacket pocket. The early morning light was a pinkish blue. The window of Room 12 still dark.

*Time for your wake-up call, motherfucker.*

# FOUR

First order of business was to check the small front parking lot to see if the Mercury station wagon was still there.

It was.

Seemed my friend had not yet checked out of his room. With any luck he was tucked in his beddy bye consorting with Wynken, Blynken and Nod. So far so good.

I headed around to the side entrance. Off-season, no breakfast was served at Wilma's Welcome Inn, and for that matter neither was lunch. The bar's food service kicked in at four PM.

This meant, when I came in loaded for bear, the front register was closed, and the only part of the place open for business was the convenience store. So the outer area—the restaurant at left, the check-out area for both hotel and bar bills at right—was underlit and unattended.

The unnumbered master key to the rooms hung on the wall of keys behind the counter, intentionally mismarked "Storage"—yes, the security at the Welcome Inn was state of the art. And only the key to Room 12 was gone.

With my left hand, I snatched the master key off its perch and headed up the flight of stairs between the closed restaurant and the front counter. My right hand, of course, remained in the pocket of the bomber jacket around the grip of the silenced nine millimeter.

The top of the stairs opened onto a hallway with doors on either side—to the guest rooms plus a couple of oversized closets for actual storage, supplies and linens and such. We only had one woman on staff, off-season, for making up rooms; and she wouldn't be in yet.

Down to the right, at the end of the hallway—the dead-end appropriately—was Room 12. I plastered my back to the wall to the left of the door and listened. For movement. For snoring. For a phone call in progress. For fucking anything.

And heard nothing.

But his fake woodie was still parked out front, so he had to still be here. Now, normally I am fairly cool—no, goddamn cool—in tense situations. But keep in mind I was accustomed to being in control of such situations—hell, I was usually the cause of them.

But for once my heart was pounding. I was trembling a little. *Goddamnit!* I was used to being in jams. I had been in plenty and talked or shot my way out. I had even dealt with threats on my home turf before—after I took the Broker out, people came looking for me, to kill me, and none of them are writing this book, are they?

Only this was different. This time I was not only the target, I was the mark. Someone had paid to have *me* killed. And I didn't like it one bit. I resented it, and it had me shaking. With rage, I think, but maybe…all right, fear. I hadn't really experienced fear like this since the earliest days in Vietnam, where I'd got numb to it fairly fast.

Two things had kept me alive in those days. First, I acted immediately to threats, no thinking, just response. Even taking a second—a fraction of a second—to process a threat can get you killed. The other thing that had kept me breathing was my sniper duty, which put me in control of such situations.

Made *me* the threat.

I calmed myself, back still to the wall. Slowed my breathing. Chilled my attitude. This fucker didn't know I was out here. Or anyway, likely didn't know.

A slight possibility existed he'd seen me out his window as I came out of the trees and across the parking lot, moving like a shark through still water. He'd have known at once I wasn't dropping by to check on the inn I owned, at least if he (or whoever hired him) knew much about me at all.

I took time to think things through, to some degree anyway. I had been up most of the night, and what little sleep I'd had was accidental. I was both wired and worn-out, a terrible combination.

*Think, Quarry, think.*

Hardly any staff on duty in the building, just the college-student gal in the convenience store. Too early for the guy who ran the filling station/garage to be in, and the pumps were all self-serve. No cleaning staff in yet. No other guests in the rooms.

That left me, outside Room 12 about to burst in and kill a guy. Shoot him in bed while he slumbered. Nobody around to hear the cough of the noise-suppressed nine mil, but the sheets would get bloody and the mattress would have an opinion, too. Simmons would almost certainly shit himself on dying—it's not an emotional reaction, it's a reflex one.

But a mess, any way you slice it.

Head shot would be messy, too, and, if he heard me and woke and sat up, would splinter the wood of the headboard. While my preference was putting one in his brain, shutting off the switch on his life, I probably needed several body shots, across the chest, to minimize mess.

If I got lucky and didn't put any bullets in the mattress—if the little killing projectiles stayed inside the guy, somewhat doubtful with a nine, but possible, bones to lodge in and such—I would still have to bundle his dead ass up in sheets and lug him the hell out of here like a rug-wrapped Cleopatra dropping in on Caesar.

Even with the world of Paradise Lake so underpopulated

this time of morning, this time of year, somebody noticing such a sight seemed like a real possibility.

*Mornin', Jack! Whatcha got there? Whatcha up to?*

*Oh, hi, Milt. Just cleanin' up after a paint job.*

*That red's a tad garish, don'tcha think?*

And then kill Milt, too. Had he existed.

Did I give a shit about any such concerns? With a contract out on me, by parties unknown but who knew about me and where I lived and Christ knew how much else, could staying in my A-frame and living my little life here be in any way salvageable?

Hard to think how.

But I did have ten grand getaway money stashed at the cottage, and the bulk of my funds were in banks here and there under the various names of my assorted identities. Easy enough to make a new start. Well, not easy, but feasible. Very damn feasible.

To hang on at Paradise Lake, though, I would have to be able to find out who hired this, and get rid of him. Or her. Or them. But just as I had worked through the Broker, Simmons almost certainly worked through an agent, a middleman, too. The purpose of that was to protect the client. Provide a buffer.

So Simmons wasn't likely to know who was behind the killing. His broker would, of course, and I might be able to get the identity of that middleman from Simmons, and work this from that end. Maybe I needed to talk to my would-be assassin, not kill him.

Or talk to him before killing him.

But did I really want to do that here? At the goddamn Welcome Inn? Could I take him captive and walk him across that parking lot over to the A-frame with my gun in his spine and fake smiles on our faces?

The thinking had calmed me, got me in a rational mode, but it hadn't given me any answers. I still had my back to the wall, literally and figuratively.

So I went back to basics. What was important now—*right now*—was surviving. The man in bed on the other side of this door, with its painted-on "12" starting to peel, was the immediate threat.

He had come onto my home ground to kill me. Meaning I needed to kill him. No other possibility presented itself. The fallout would be handled when it came.

The jury in my mind was unanimous: killing Simmons was the first order of business. Maybe I could locate the backup man, the passive prick on this hit, and get the name of their broker out of him. What I needed from the active asshole was for him not to be breathing anymore.

And my breathing? It was calm. Right now, it was calm again.

All I had to do now was work the key in the door. A few feet inside the room would put me at the foot of the double bed where he probably still slept. If he was up and out of bed, the mirrored dresser would be at my left, a closet at the near side of the dresser. The bathroom was off to the right. Number 12, like the rest of the rooms at the Welcome Inn, was modest. Small. Not like the accommodations at the former Playboy Club in Geneva. Vacationers with limited funds stayed here. In season.

Few stayed here now, and even Simmons was about to check out....

While I'm not technically ambidextrous, the various situations I've found myself in have given me unusual skills. Lip-reading, for one. Using my left hand almost as well as my right is another.

With my left, I worked the key, the lock clicked, that hand

was on the knob and twisting, and I was in, fast, kicking the door shut behind me with a heel, staying low, but not so low that I couldn't put a couple of silenced slugs into the torso of a sleeping man.

Only the bed was empty of anything but slept-in sheets, blankets and pillows.

Nobody at left, by the dresser, either. I rolled to the right, to the open door of the little bathroom, where the tub was empty, the shower curtain back. Nor was anyone taking a shit, dead or alive.

On my hands and knees I checked under the bed, like a husband desperate to prove his wife was cheating on him, and saw nothing but evidence I was paying the woman too much who cleaned here.

That left only the closet at the left of the dresser. I considered putting a few bullets into that door, expense be damned, but had Simmons been hiding (or waiting) in there, surely he would have taken the opportunity to shoot my ass while I was crawling around on the floor checking up on the cleaning staff.

I checked out the guest room thoroughly. No canvas travel bag. Empty dresser drawers. He'd bathed or showered already. No toiletries in the john. Nothing but hangers and a spare pillow in the closet. Nothing at all to show he'd been here, except his room key, left on the dresser top.

I sat on an edge of the unmade bed, the nine mil in my hand draped in my lap like a limp dick.

*What the fuck?*

Exits at either end of the upstairs hall made it possible he'd slipped out just as I was coming in. But, shit—what was this, a French farce?

*What the hell did this mean?*

No. Not the right question.

*Where is he now?*

Better question.

I took the stairs at the opposite end of the hall, which was the quickest way down to the convenience store. This emptied right into the little parking lot at the front of the building, where the station wagon was no longer parked.

*Shit!*

The gal behind the convenience store counter, a black girl who was cute and a little heavy in a nice way, sat back behind the register and point-of-purchase displays reading a Stephen King paperback. Her name was Carrie, but that wasn't the title of the book. She looked up pleasantly.

"You're an early bird, Jack."

Everybody here called me by my first name. I was a boss who didn't stand on ceremony. A lovable son of a bitch.

"Yeah, any business this morning?"

She got up and came over to her counter. Her University of Wisconsin sweatshirt was gray with red letters with the Bucky Badger mascot swaggering between its formidable contents.

"Hardly any," she said, leaning an elbow. "Guy bought some cigarettes is all."

"What did he look like?"

She shrugged. "Just a guy. Dark hair? Pointy features, kinda?"

I nodded. "Dressed how?"

"Overcoat, I guess. Gray? He asked when we opened for breakfast and I said late April. I don't think that's what he meant."

"Probably not," I said, and managed a little smile.

"He wanted to know where he could get breakfast and I told him Marv's."

That was a diner in Twin Lakes, not far from here.

"Gave him directions," she went on with a shrug. "Said they'd be open. Six AM, they open."

I nodded. "Thanks, Carrie."

"Any problem, Jack?"

"No. Just a guest who left something in his room. Thought maybe I could catch up with him."

"Well, if it's important, he could be at Marv's. I mean, he got directions."

I smiled and nodded.

"Not important at all," I said.

Marv's, in nearby Twin Lakes, had an enviable view on Lake Mary. In summer, they always had a line down the block and nobody minded. But things right now were so slow, I had no trouble parking right out front—no Mercury station wagon taking up a space, either. I'd already checked the small parking lot in back, which had a few cars, but no fake woodie.

I just sat there in the Impala a while, wondering whether I should drive around looking for Simmons and his ride outside some other restaurant. But Marv's was about it for Twin Lakes right now. There'd be more options if I drove the twenty miles to Lake Geneva, but was that the right move?

Shaking my head at this frustrating shit, I stepped out into surprising cold. Despite my bomber jacket, the morning chill cut through me like a knife. A sharp one. I hadn't noticed the cold snap when I clipped across that parking lot earlier. I guess I'd been distracted by the thought of kill or be killed.

I went inside. This time of year, the locals hardly put a dent in Marv's booths, tables and counter seating. The building had been a private home once upon a time, but the lower floor had been a diner and kitchen going back to the '40s. The walls were cheap paneling with framed local sports pages, religious images, and Bears pics hanging crooked cheek to askew jowl. Big mounted shellacked fish hung here and there. That kind of thing never made me want to order the catch of the day.

I sat at the counter. A skinny waitress named Hazel, who

had been here since the Depression, and still seemed pretty depressed, came over and squeezed out a smile. Her hair had never been blonde but still was.

"Usual, Jack?"

"Sure." The kitchen sink omelet, ingredients varying day to day. "Put the order in and come back, would you, beautiful?"

"Anything for you, honey."

Rumor had it she'd been through several husbands, all of whom had lived off her. You had to wonder about a guy content to live off a waitress. How could you respect a guy who couldn't find a woman with a better-paying job?

She put my order in at the window—mustached Marv was doing the cooking himself, no help back there off-season—and then she brought me a Diet Coke. She knew I didn't drink coffee. I sipped the pop while she lingered, to see what it was I wanted of her. Also, I was one of maybe half a dozen customers. All local, of course. So she didn't have much else to do.

I asked, "Anybody in today you didn't recognize?"

"Nope."

"You sure? Guy about my size, my age, but not as good-looking?"

"We get those all the time, honey."

"Kinda pointy nose. Pointy chin."

She was shaking her head. "Nobody in here so far today that I had to bother askin' what they want."

"Regulars."

"Regulars." She leaned on the counter. Somewhere in that creped face hid pretty features that should have given her a better life. "You asking for any special reason, Jack?"

"No." I figured I better keep the same story going. "Guest at the Inn left something in his room. Hoped to catch him. Our girl Carrie at the grocery said she recommended this place to him for breakfast."

"Nice of her. The little colored girl, right?"

"Right." She wasn't that little, but right.

Hazel shrugged. "I never had any trouble with her."

Nobody had, but people said things like that around here.

A bell dinged and she went to the window, then brought me my omelet. She seemed like maybe she'd keep lingering, so I smiled and nodded and carted my eggs and Diet Coke off to a corner table to think. No, to ruminate. That's the word.

So Simmons had asked "the colored girl" where to get breakfast, got directions here, then hadn't used them. Either that, or he didn't like the looks of the place and drove on by.

But Marv's looked clean enough from outside, and from within—if he'd stopped and stuck his head in—seemed no better nor worse than your usual eccentric local eatery. And the food smells were pleasant enough.

Whatever. He hadn't stopped here.

But had he driven on past?

Had I scoped this out all wrong? Maybe we were talking about that rare specimen, the genuine, sure-enough, honest-to-God coincidence. Maybe Simmons was on his way to a job upstate that had nothing to do with me. Maybe he had just happened to stop at Wilma's Welcome Inn to spend the night somewhere quiet and out-of-the-way.

Was it possible I wasn't the target at all?

Simmons was certainly not acting like the backup half of a hit team. You don't do one day's surveillance and then split. Of course, Simmons might be working the active side, and had stayed a night at the Inn at the direction of the passive partner, to get a room with a view on the scene of the coming crime. That made *some* sense....

Not much, though. What I would have done—following a procedure I knew others in the trade plied—was check in with my partner and go over the intel he'd gathered. Do some final planning. Coordinate with my partner. Determine whether the passive half could split or needed to stick around and provide literal backup.

Possibly that was what Simmons was doing right now.

Making contact with his stakeout guy to put the finishing touches on my finish.

I finished the Diet Coke but left half the omelet behind, paid Hazel at the register and headed to Paradise Lake, not sure what my next move should be. Also not sure what Simmons and his nameless partner's next moves might be.

Still in the Impala, I drove back to my A-frame. No car was parked along the lane, and the gravel apron in front of the deck revealed no guests, either. I sat for a moment in the car, my thoughts doing their best not to go too fast or too far. What were my options?

It was doubtful Simmons would be waiting inside. Either he had not come to my turf with me in mind, and had driven on to his real job, as opposed to the one I'd imagined for him; or he would wait till nightfall. Middle of the night, most likely. If I was the target, that meant somebody knew who and what I was, and you don't confront a professional killer head on. You sneak up, you surprise, or…

…shoot him from a distance.

With all those empty cabins and cottages hugging the lake, a sniper finding a suitable position for some artistry with a high-powered rifle would be a fucking snap.

Should I run from the car to the house, to make a running target? But that would tip my assassins to my knowledge of their existence and the job they'd come to do.

Bad move.

Of course, not as bad as just making myself a casual easy shot by sauntering up the steps to the deck and in the door. The best I could do was split the difference—move quickly but not suspiciously.

And I would make the best target when I paused to use my key. If I were in those woods across the way with a sniper-scope rifle, that's when I'd do it, and the fucker in my sights would not have a chance in hell.

So I changed things up.

I got out of the Impala, quick but not frantic, and did not go up the steps to the deck. Instead, acting like there was something I had to do—*which was true: stay alive*—I cut back alongside the A-frame to the rear door and used my house key, already in my left hand, quickly and efficiently.

And went in.

For what seemed like the thousandth time, I moved carefully through my A-frame with the silenced nine mil in hand and checked everywhere. Yes, even under the beds.

The place was clear.

Last night, keeping the drapes shut made sense. This time of day it didn't. I wanted to see what was coming. Who was coming. So I drew open the drapes, revealing my picture postcard view of the lake, sun shimmering gold on the water, sky blue with cotton ball clouds, with only the dark trees, dead-looking ones mingling with evergreens, to remind me of reality.

All the thinking had got me tired. That and the no sleep last night. I figured I'd need to spend the day in here, the evening too, waiting. Waiting for company.

So I prepped by piling some furniture in front of the back door, kitchenette chairs, tables and such. Blocked paths that would trip up an invader, should he come through a window, or at least make him reveal himself by noise. Even spread some bubble-pack on the floor under bedroom windows.

Not that I would fall asleep. By God, I would stay awake. I'd started the caffeine regimen with that Diet Coke at breakfast. I brought a whole six-pack back from the fridge.

I got a fire going, which prompted me to get out of the bomber jacket, and I moved the sectional couch pieces around so I could have my feet up and the gun in my lap as I lay back against the comfy cushion. I had an extra ammo magazine for the nine mil on the cushion next to me. I'd removed the silencer, which made the weapon too bulky for combat situations.

Didn't dare put music on or the TV or read a book. I needed to stay alert. No distractions. Just the shimmer of lake and blue of sky, with enough light coming in to help keep me from nodding off. It took me back to the sniper days in country, where I might sit watch for hours on end, waiting for somebody to kill. Sometimes a specific somebody.

I was ready.

"Wake up," a voice said.

Simmons.

Training my silenced nine mil on me.

# FIVE

I sat up.

Not a sudden movement. Very slow and careful, and some part of my brain was wondering if this could be a dream, which is to say nightmare, but it wasn't.

This was all too real.

Bruce Simmons was seated on a backless section of the sectional facing me, his somewhat pointed features lending him a satanic cast, as did a widow's peak I hadn't noticed before on the product-heavy dark hair, longer than mine. His position was edge of his seat, leaning just a little forward. I was slumped, which was why I needed to straighten some.

Falling asleep was unprofessional, if human, and I can credit myself only for snapping awake immediately, going instantly alert, the way you are if you hear somebody trying to break into your house or hotel room.

Of course I hadn't heard him actually breaking in, had I? So I didn't have much to brag about. And I had no idea how he'd got himself inside, maneuvering around my bubble-pack and furniture blockades, and didn't really care. That was beside the point now, wasn't it?

On the other hand, I'd been deep enough asleep that my guest had risked setting the stage some. The drapes on the double doors onto the deck and the lake were now closed. The square of cushioned sectional he was perched on was backed away from me enough to avoid a kick at his gun-in-hand or anything else for that matter.

And, as I said, he was aiming my own nine-millimeter automatic at me. The extra ammo clip he had confiscated and tucked away somewhere. He was out of his topcoat and wearing a black track suit with white stripes down the sleeves and legs. If he was here to force me into dressing like that, he'd have to shoot me.

I'd fallen asleep in the clothes I'd worn since yesterday and through the night, jeans and a long-sleeve navy t-shirt. I'd like to tell you I had a throwing knife or small revolver tucked at the small of my back, but I didn't.

The only thing I had going for me was that I was alive. That he hadn't killed me while I slept, which is what I deserved; but I'd only been awake maybe two seconds before I realized he was here for more than fulfilling a contract.

"Wondering why you're still alive?" he asked. He had a baritone voice that would have gone well with a gig as a late-night jazz-spinning disc jockey. Soothing, almost, except for the part where he was a hired killer holding my own gun on me.

"I am," I admitted. "Pleasantly so."

"Thing is, I know who you are." Smug. Proud of himself.

"If you didn't," I said, "this would be random, and you don't look nuts to me. And I'm not just trying to get on your good side."

His mouth twitched a smile. His dark eyes were hooded, which added to the vaguely sinister effect of the sharp if handsome features. Reminded me of the old movie actor Zachary Scott. Same oily smoothness.

"When I say I know who you are," he said, "I mean I *know* who you *are*...Quarry."

What did he want, applause? Or maybe for me to start shaking? I'd already done enough shaking for this prick, waiting outside his room at Wilma's and he hadn't even been in it. Fuck this guy.

"Is that right," I said politely, "Mr. Simmons?"

The eyes weren't hooded now.

"How do you know who *I* am?" he demanded, some edge in the disc-jockey baritone.

My turn for smug. "Is that really what you want to talk about? How we know who we are?"

He sat back just a little, but no couch was behind him to lean on. "You worked for the Broker. I did, too, a long time ago. That must be how you know me."

"Must be how *you* know *me*. What next? And, uh, by the way—I didn't work for the Broker." I tapped my chest. "He worked for me. He was my agent."

Simmons nodded in irritation, said, "Of course. I work through the Envoy."

I had to laugh. "Christ, not a very imaginative bunch in this business, are they?"

He seemed vaguely offended. "There are a number of agents, brokers, in our game. They each have kind of…code name. Designating regions." He gestured a little with the hand with my gun in it, not threatening, really—just gesturing. "Didn't you know that?"

I shrugged, not putting much into it, not wanting to get shot. "Not really. I figured as much, but, no."

I obviously knew the assassins on Broker's roll call all had one-word aliases, and figured that was to keep real names or traceable fake ones off phone calls and other communications. That the same was true of other middlemen in the killing game came as no surprise.

And, of course, I knew what Simmons' own wry little Broker-invented "code name" was—Brace. Something or somebody you could lean on. But it was also a synonym for "crutch," wasn't it?

I would keep that knowledge to myself, however—no need to show off, or show my hand.

I asked, "When somebody killed the Broker, did they divvy

up his merry little band of butchers? Or did somebody take over as, what…regional manager?"

He was getting pissed off, which was fine by me, because that's part of what I was going for—unsettling him.

"I'm asking the fucking questions, Quarry!…Another broker took over, yes. But some…talent…went elsewhere. That's part of how you got away with it for so long."

"Got away with what?"

"Whatever it is you've been doing. There are theories."

I raised my eyebrows. "What does the 'Envoy' think? Do you two talk in his secret lair? Use the Cone of Silence, maybe?"

His eyebrows, on the other hand, furrowed. "Do you want to die, Quarry?"

"Not particularly. Not today. What is it you think I've done? Theories about what?"

He shifted a little on the cushion. We were around the campfire now.

"Since the Broker's murder, almost ten years ago," Simmons said, "something odd has been happening. Took a while to make itself clear—for a pattern to emerge out of you doing whatever it is you're doing. But it finally did, and you might have got away with it, if you had only pursued this…" He shrugged. "…project of yours for a few years. Or perhaps only indulged yourself once a year."

"Oh, I indulge myself practically every day. I subscribe to *Hustler* magazine. I even have the occasional hot fudge sundae."

He let that slide. "We're not exactly sure how you've gone about it, or even why, or whether it's a moneymaking enterprise or just some kind of…. We've speculated you are trying to atone for what you did, in your years working for the Broker."

I started to laugh, genuinely laugh. "Stop. You're killing me. Atone? Jesus!"

Simmons was working hard at staying calm. At not taking the bait. I would rate his results as just fair.

He said, "Took more than a couple of years for anybody to notice. But the talent roster kept getting thinned—people like us, Quarry, out in the field on a job, started dying mysteriously. Violently. And contracts got cancelled, after…when the clients *themselves* got cancelled. Also violently."

I risked another little shrug. "I suppose once the client is out of the picture, so is the contract. Point becomes moot. What does that have to do with me?"

He was studying me but not getting anywhere. "All of the teams whose efforts have been disrupted—all of those killed out in the field under those violent, mysterious circumstances—once worked for the Broker. This strange, slow epidemic, which has raged on for damn near a decade, has not touched the other regions in any major way. But it got noticed, Quarry. Whatever it is you did, that you're doing, it got noticed. You shouldn't have been greedy."

I held out an open palm. "Let's say you're right. Let's say this Envoy character has valid suspicions, although you must admit they're vague. What you do for a living—what *I* used to do for a living—it's dangerous work. A man can get killed."

"He can," Simmons agreed.

"But I would be willing to assure you and, through you, assure your Envoy that I am happily settled here with a good, prosperous little business…I have a restaurant lodge I run, not far from here—maybe you noticed it? I have no desire to give that business up or my quiet life here, and will guarantee you and your business associate that I am not interested in doing anything else. Certainly nothing involving my previous…career. I won't be hard to find. You can come back and plug me at your convenience. Isn't that fair?"

Now he smiled. A sudden calm came over him and his smile became a narrow, reptilian thing.

"You misunderstand me, Quarry. Mind if I smoke?"

He could fucking burn, as far as I was concerned.

"Not at all," I said. "Use the fireplace as an ashtray."

"Thanks." He'd worked up some ambidextrous skills, too, in his time; he got out a deck of Marlboros from a track suit pocket—must have liked to have a smoke while he jogged—and a lighter, too. Got a cigarette going.

I never smoked. That shit can kill you.

"Oh, the Envoy sent me to take you out, all right," Simmons said cheerfully. We were just two guys in the same line of work swapping war stories now. "But I have my own agenda."

"That right?"

He nodded. "I've been doing this work a long time. Since I got back from Vietnam. You served, right?"

"Yes."

"Marine, wasn't it?"

"Semper fi, Mac."

"Sorry. I was regular army." He let smoke out of his lungs to pollute my living room. "I've been at this over a dozen years."

"Long time."

"Too damn long. Few years ago I met a nice woman and something inside of me…rekindled."

Maybe it was the smoking.

He went on: "Something human woke up in me. I met a girl in a bar. Not a girl, no—a young woman. Smart, funny, nice, beautiful."

"Congratulations."

"We have a kid. Little boy. Looks like me, they say."

I hadn't noticed.

"Anyway, I don't want to be out playing with guns like this

anymore." He gestured with my nine mil in hand again. "I've had it with that shit."

"So go straight."

He made a face. "And do fucking what? You think I got a college degree over in the Nam? I own a little business, but I can't live the way I want from it. And I don't want to get killed in the line of duty, either, particularly since that duty is just wasting some cheating wife or crooked business partner or mob guy when they want somebody from outside to do their dirty work."

"Tell me about it."

This time he offered up the one-shoulder shrug. "So I need something lucrative. And you can help me on that score."

"I can?"

"You can. I am even willing to cut you in for a healthy taste. Twenty-five percent just for sitting here in your nice cottage on this nice lake."

On my nice ass. Right. That would happen.

"Twenty-five percent," I asked, "of what?"

"I figure you have names. Addresses. Information. All these brokers around the country have that shit. The Broker certainly had it. I figure that's what you've been using, the Broker's list."

*Uh-oh*, like some long-dead lady on the *I Love Lucy* laugh track always said.

Simmons went on: "I don't know exactly how you're using the list, and I don't care. But I know how *I* would use it."

He didn't go into that, though.

Finally I said, "Let's say I know what you're talking about. Just hypothetically."

"Let's," he said.

"How—exactly—would you use this list?"

"Is that your concern?"

"If I get twenty-five percent it is." Of course he had no intention of doing that, but I had to play along.

He mulled it some, or pretended to. Then he sat forward and almost whispered, as if we were in public and not in my living room.

"Okay, Quarry—I'll really give you an opportunity. Ground-floor kinda deal. See, I know where the Envoy keeps his information. Very old-fashioned fella, the Envoy. Wall safe at home. His list of names, merged with the names you have, would be very lucrative."

I nodded slightly, eyes narrowed, getting it, yet managing not to laugh at this shit. So he wanted out of the killing business, and his way of doing that was to become a magnate of murder, with an expansive stable of professional killers and an ongoing relationship with organized crime. The better to make a nice life for the little woman and his boy.

Beautiful.

I leaned forward, just a shade, and my eyes locked onto his. "You may have something there. But we have to find a way for me to trust you. And for you to trust me. Any ideas?"

"Absolutely," he said, and I slapped the nine mil from his hand and the gun flew past the shag carpet and into the kitchenette where it skittered on the tile. This I heard, not saw, as I was diving for him, taking him back over the section of couch onto the floor.

He hit hard with me on top of him, but he reacted fast, getting a hand under my chin and shoving me off and back, where I clanged into the metal fireplace, feeling the heat. I crumpled in on myself and he hit me in the jaw, dropping me to the shag. He looked toward the kitchenette, apparently having seen where the nine mil went, and was on his way there, hunkered like a tackle looking for a quarterback to cripple, but I kicked him in the ass with the flat of my running shoe, shoving him back down to the floor again. Him on his belly, like a flopping fish on deck, gave me a less than ideal path to his balls, but his legs were apart enough that I could send the toe of a shoe between and under his ass cheeks.

His howl meant I'd judged right, and then while he was busy screaming, I went past him to retrieve my nine mil, which was resting by the cabinets under the sink.

But then he was on me, even as he whimpered from the gonad goal I'd kicked, and hugged me from behind, around the waist, like he was going to fuck me whether I wanted him to or not. He had my arms pinned and I hadn't made it to the nine mil, so we were locked in a kind of awkward dance there in the small area.

Suddenly he let me go and his hands came up and fingers gripped my either ear and he slammed my head into the kitchenette counter. That left me reeling, all but unconscious, and he had the nine mil again and dragged me into the living room and threw me on the floor.

I looked up at him. And down the barrel of the silenced nine mil.

He was breathing hard, but then so was I.

He came down on top of me, shoving a knee in my stomach—apparently he was in no mood to get kicked in the balls again—and I turned my head to one side and puked up some of my breakfast.

Again, I could only think of a rapist as he held me down, kind of sitting on me, knee in my belly, gun snout in my face. He was as out of breath as I was. "Where…where's…the…fucking…list?"

"Not…here."

"Don't…fucking…lie…to me…."

"Tear...the place...up. Go for it."

"Where is...*is* it, then?"

"Bank. Safe deposit...box."

"Then there's...a key. We'll get...get the key...and go...go to the bank."

"Never...never mind."

"What?"

"The list...*is* here."

He grinned, said "Good," then the cough of a silenced handgun made me think, momentarily, he'd accidentally shot me.

But that wasn't it.

His eyes were wide—not at all hooded—and a gaping hole in his forehead spewed brains, bone and blood on my already puke-flecked face, while a projectile whizzed over my scalp, practically parting my hair.

Somebody came over and yanked the dead weight off of me. I sat up, blinking. Somebody ran water. Somebody brought me a towel. I cleaned my face off. Looked up at who had saved me.

A beautiful woman in a forest-green jumpsuit loomed, too slender for her voluptuous breasts, her almost Asian eyes dark and staring.

"Hello, Jack," she said.

"Hello, Lu," I said.

# SIX

*Glenna Cole was the name she used at first.*
*Ivy was what the Broker called her.*
*Lucille was how she introduced herself when we met.*
*Lu?*
*That was what I called her.*

Ten years ago or so, when I came into possession of the Broker's list, ready to make my first attempt to follow a professional killer to an intended victim, I selected from that list the name Glenna Cole/Ivy. I'm not sure I could tell you why I zeroed in on one of the handful of women on the Broker's team.

But I did.

Maybe I figured a female would be easier to handle, to control, to overpower, physically. The emotional side never occurred to me. How foolish are the young.

Or I might have been challenging myself to see if I had it in me to dispatch a woman with the same dispassion I routinely brought to my other assignments. I'd never killed a woman before, except in self-defense a few times.

Anyway, for whatever reason, Glenna Cole was the name I settled on, which led me to a "swinging singles" apartment complex in Florida. Maybe that was another factor in my choice of Broker's "Ivy"—the opportunity to exchange the Midwest cold for some fun and sun. A vacation with pay, right?

Stupid.

Right.

Ivy, of course, was a name typical of the cute, droll monikers the Broker bestowed upon those of us on his roster—referencing poison ivy, probably. Or it could have referred to Lu's tenacity, her ability to cling to her marks.

Or maybe he was alluding to her seductive qualities, indicating she used her charms as a means to get close to a target. But if that were the case, I never knew about it.

In Florida, I'd kept my distance, having ingratiated myself with another bikini-resplendent resident of the Beach Shore Apartments, inhabited mostly by youngish divorcees flush with alimony—stewardesses and waitresses who got lucky with rich old fucks.

This led to the males being the sex objects at the redundantly named Beach Shore, specimens usually five or ten years younger than the females. I had so much sex with Nancy Who's-It, my dick got red and I wondered if I'd caught something.

Glenna Cole probably had five years on my twenty-five at the time. But otherwise she hadn't at all fit the pattern of the sun bunnies of the Beach Shore. Her hair was dark blonde and shoulder-brushing, fairly standard here. Her face was a narrow oval, her nose thin and long, her eyes large and almond-shaped, an Asian cast.

That mouth of hers, under that slightly beaky nose, seemed too wide, and her gums showed when she smiled. She was taller than my five ten by at least an inch. Her legs were on the skinny side and she lacked the narrow waist of the classic hourglass beauty. Her breasts were large enough to overwhelm her tall, slender frame.

And yet.

She had easily been the most strikingly beautiful female among the many bikini babes at the Beach Shore. Those Asian eyes were dark blue, flecked gold. That bosom rode full and high and proud. And she carried herself with a confidence that was the glue putting all the disparate elements together, which added up to one lovely goddamn woman.

Down at the Beach Shore, I had never spoken to her. Never locked eyes with her. I was on surveillance, after all. I was in full beard, trimmed enough to not look like a hobo but still conceal the planes of my face; that, and constant Ray-Bans, did the trick. Plus, I was hiding in the anonymity of one tanned healthy body after another tanned healthy body, female and male, a sexual buffet at this swinger's paradise.

At all times I did my best to keep the pool between Glenna Cole and me, but once or twice she climbed out of the water dripping, right in front of me, her flimsy top slipping down to tease with dark circles of areola. Her unique features and bosomy height made quite the droplet-pearled sight, which of course I pretended not to see.

But I saw, all right. And there was something about her that wasn't purely physical.

Something that made a man want to fuck her, sure, but more than that want to *know* her, in more than the Biblical sense. Before long I was regretting choosing her name from the Broker's list. There were any number of things I would have liked to do with her, and to her, but killing her wasn't one of them.

And I almost certainly would have to.

This new enterprise I was attempting required eliminating the threat to my client, once I determined who that client might be, of course. That meant two kills, the passive and active players both; three, if I could discover who took out the contract. Back in the Broker days, all I had to do on a job was wipe out a single measly human.

Beard shaved off, I followed Glenna Cole AKA Ivy out of the sun and across the country into the cold and a cornfield casino in the Heartland, where she had arranged a job as a waitress in close proximity to her target. I got to know her, first as a customer and then as a fellow employee, and we hit it off. We dated. Mated. Just two people who casually connected.

Or so I assumed, unless maybe she had seen past the now absent facial hair and sunglasses and recalled me from the Beach Shore. In that event, I was the one in danger.

But as things worked out, it seemed she really hadn't tipped to having seen me before, although I had made a crucial mistake by assuming she was working the active half of the assignment. She was in fact in passive mode, surveilling the mark, and this misstep on my part almost got the client killed.

Live and learn.

One positive result, though, had been my ability to approach the hit team's target and convince him of the danger he was in, and that I wasn't some crank or con man or just plain lunatic. As my first attempt at making the Broker's list work for me, it had gone well. I was on to something.

And, as it happened, I was able to bring the job to a resolution without having to kill the woman with the Asian eyes and large breasts. A happy outcome. Like they say, win-win.

What I had not expected was that I'd bond with Lu in a way that would feel real. That I'd come quickly to like her. Feel real affection for her. And that she would at least *seem* to feel the same about me.

How that all played out has been recounted elsewhere, but I can give you this much.

Once her partner was killed under apparently accidental circumstances—and after the party who took out the murder contract had himself been removed (by me, of course)—Lu had nothing left to do but move on. We had never discussed who we really were in all this. I sensed she suspected I was responsible for both the contract, and her partner, going belly up. But, if so, that remained unspoken of.

We left on good if ambiguous terms, though there had been nothing ambiguous about the hot and heavy hump that had been our frantic goodbye.

After that, I asked her to come along with me, not even knowing what exactly I was asking, possibly thinking that together we might have a chance at some other way of life.

But her response had been, "Maybe next time," and she'd gone.

In almost ten years, no "next time" had come.

Now, unexpectedly, it had.

"Let's get you up," Lu said, and she had her gun in one hand—a Glock nine mil with a noise suppressor longer than its barrel—and held my left arm at the elbow with the other. Her hair was blonder now, and ponytailed back.

But I would have known her anywhere, let alone in my living room with a silenced Glock.

She had already dragged me out from under what used to be Bruce Simmons, who was face down on my shag carpet, a little red *bindi*-like hole on the wrong side of his head.

Steadying myself, with her help, I said, "I'm lucky that bullet didn't hit me in the face."

She gave me half a smile. "Would've bounced off like Superman. Lost its velocity making the trip. Hiding somewhere in the shag now—I'll find it later. You want to sit down?"

I nodded.

Lu sat next to me on a couch sectional, as far away from the corpse on the floor as we could manage without leaving the room. The Glock she tossed on another section nearby. This was a part of the couch where you could lean back, and I did.

"We have a mess to clean up," she said.

We weren't talking about how she had happened to save my ass—my life—or why she was here. I already knew she must have been the late Simmons' partner. That she was his surveillance half and likely had been on the other end of the binoculars across the way in a certain cabin last night.

And she knew that I knew. Some things between a man and a woman don't need saying. As for why she shot him and not me, I figured we'd get around to that. I wasn't incredibly focused yet.

"Limited mess," I said with a shrug. "Dead men don't bleed. Maybe you noticed that before."

Her eyebrows went up. "Be that as it may, we still have a dead body to deal with. At least he didn't shit himself."

"Small favors."

The fingers of her right hand moved tentatively into my scalp. "You have blood and brains in your hair. Why don't you take a shower?"

"Why don't I?"

I got up and she took my arm and I said, "I'm fine."

"No, you're shaking."

"Fuck I am. I'm *fine*. Just got a little knocked around, is all, and then splattered."

"Worse ways to get splattered," she observed.

"Definitely."

She walked me to the bathroom anyway. As I was stripping down, she asked if I had anything to wrap her partner up in.

"Sure," I said, and told her where the supplies were in one of the rooms under the loft overhang. "Plastic sheeting—drop cloth. Should be a roll of duct tape on a shelf."

She nodded and went off.

I took a long hot shower. Washed my hair, really washed it. Blood like that cakes and brains are worse. I was in the cubicle long enough, surrounded by steam, to wonder if I had imagined the last hour or so. Maybe I'd been dreaming. Maybe I was still asleep.

But when I turned off the water and stepped out to towel off, hot water replaced with cold air, I realized I was awake, all right.

In the master bedroom I got into fresh clothes, including another long-sleeve t-shirt and jeans and back into the Reeboks. When I joined her in the living room, my beautiful guest in the forest-green jumpsuit had wrapped the dead fucker up in plastic and sealed the deal with duct tape, really cocooned the guy. She was wearing little white gloves, like this was 1958 and she was Audrey Hepburn. On the other hand, she was in Reeboks, too.

Lu looked down at her handiwork, pleased.

"Nice job," I said.

"Thanks." The Asian eyes had their way with me. "May I make a suggestion?"

"Why not?"

She gestured at the plastic package. "We shouldn't dump him till after dark. Even though it's pretty dead around here. You have any ideas?"

I nodded. "Plenty of gravel pits in the area."

"Filled with water?"

I nodded again. "And still frozen over."

She frowned. "That a problem?"

"Don't think so. That package should break the ice and submerge just fine. Is his station wagon around somewhere?"

Her head bobbed. "Halfway down your lane."

"What did you come in?"

A shrug. "Just a car I bought for the job."

Nothing had been said yet about how I *was* the job.

"Used Camaro," she added. "Lot of miles, a few dings, but still a nice ride. Let's put him in the station wagon. After dark, I mean."

I'd been right that a woodie like that could come in handy.

She edged over to me and smiled, one old friend to another. Put a hand on my shoulder. "Jack, you look beat. Uh, you *are* Jack here, right?"

"Yeah, I'm Jack. I told you I'm fine."

She flipped a hand toward the floor. "Look, I can babysit the mummy here while you catch some z's. I'll wake you when it's dark enough out."

"No. I don't want to sleep till this is dealt with."

"Till the body's dumped."

"Right. I know just the right gravel pit. There's a downhill slope to a drop-off. I can jump out and it'll just keep going. Right through the ice and gone."

"Cool. Kind of in your back yard, though."

I shrugged. "Mob bodies get dumped around here all the time. Won't come back on me."

"Good." She looked me over sympathetically. "Can't sleep, huh?"

"Won't sleep."

She frowned in thought. "Could you eat?"

I nodded. "Yeah."

Now that I'd washed my hair I could.

"How's the food at that place you own?"

She'd been the surveillance half of the team, all right.

I said, "Limited menu but damn good. You like chili?"

"Who doesn't, in this weather?"

"Let's walk it."

We did. We did not hold hands or anything. A near decade had passed, after all, and our relationship had been a short one.

Plus, she may well have figured out I was behind that contract going south in Des Moines, all those years ago. And that I had been the one responsible for her partner, the active half of the team, meeting a "shocking fate," as the *Register* put it.

Walking close enough for our shoulders to brush now and then, our breaths smoking with the cold, we exchanged a few vaguely embarrassed grins. Before long we were seated in a booth in the corner of the bar of the Inn, waiting for our chili to arrive. Charley was behind the bar, giving me the "who's the babe?" fish-eye.

Lu was sipping a Bloody Mary and I was working on a Diet Coke. Suddenly things felt a little awkward.

Her chin crinkled with a smile.

"So," she said. "What's new?"

# SEVEN

Late afternoon at Wilma's Welcome Inn, in the bar, was not exactly hopping. A couple of locals who worked in Geneva but lived in Paradise Lake were chatting and drinking, with Charley wiping down the counter and cleaning glasses, pretending to work since the boss was around.

Lu and I ate our chili with the conversation limited at first to how good it was. Her inquiry about what was new got this response from me: "Not much."

Meanwhile I was mulling, as I imagine she was, exactly what we should talk about here in public. Not much chance of anything being overheard, with just Charley and those locals around, although Brenda had stuck her head in, arriving for work. She frowned at me, as if I were her husband she'd caught running around, and disappeared, presumably getting back behind the register a wall away.

Lu and I both decided, without discussing it, that our conversation should be limited to the lives we led away from homicidal work pursuits. Our "real" lives. Or was that fake ones?

She paused with a spoonful of chili waiting midair for her attention. "How did you end up here, Jack?"

"I've been in that A-frame for years," I said. "Going on fifteen."

"No kidding."

I nodded. Swallowed chili—I didn't let the kitchen vary from Wilma's recipe by a grain of spice. "I was given a generous advance by a businessman who took me on."

"I may know him," she said innocently. Another delicate bite of chili. "He was a broker, wasn't he?"

*There it was, out in the open. Or anyway, out in the open behind the bushes. She had come in on her partner about to kill me and had chosen to kill him instead—why, I didn't know, other than my native charm.*

"That's right," I said. "Oh, I forgot. You worked with him, too. The Broker."

She didn't miss a beat. "But what got you into the hotel and restaurant business?"

I shrugged, broke a couple of crackers in my chili. "Just drifted into it. This inn was just a place near where I lived, and I took a lot of meals here and got friendly with the people. There really was a Wilma, once."

"Not just a name starting with 'w' to go with Welcome Inn?"

"Not at all. Big gal, kind of sexy in her way. I liked the hell out of Wilma."

"What became of her?"

"She passed away." Well, really, she got shoved down those stairs out there, by somebody I killed later. "And I ended up buying the place."

Very softly she said, "Good money laundry, I bet."

"It is. Makes *real* dough in season, though. Paradise Lake hasn't been commercialized like Twin Lakes and Geneva. Wilma's is one of a handful of places in town near the lake itself that's zoned for dining and lodging."

"Aren't you the little businessman."

"What about you, Lu? It is still 'Lu,' isn't it?"

The wide mouth twitched in a smile. "It always will be, to you."

We each had a little more chili, then I asked her, "What's your story? What have you been up to? What's your life like these days?"

She smiled, sighed, shrugged. "I've been in St. Paul for the last seven years or so. I have an antique shop. Specialize in '30s, '40s, '50s modern. Good-size operation. We have auctions, I do appraisals."

"I bet it requires occasional travel."

Another twitch of a smile. "It does. Do you travel much?"

"Less than I used to. Significant other?"

She spooned her chili, as if looking for a diamond hidden in there. Then: "Had a few of those. Hard to manage, with my... travel. My interests. Compartmentalizing is hard."

"Yeah it is."

"Sometimes I think...."

"What do you think, sometimes?"

She looked up. "Sometimes I think I need to find somebody who can relate to some of the...odder things that have occupied my time, and interests."

"I hear that."

She leaned in, just a little. "You remember what I told you about my husband?"

"He ran a nightclub somewhere, didn't he?"

She nodded. "Detroit. I tended bar for him. He liked having a good-looking young woman doing that. The men liked it."

"I'm sure they did."

"Do you remember how he...passed away?"

"I do."

I actually didn't, not the details anyway. All I knew was he'd been embezzling from his mobbed-up silent partners, and those silent partners got vocal about it. Him being dead was the gist.

"How about you, Jack?"

"How about what?"

"Do you have a significant other? Other than that twat who stuck her head in and gave us a dirty look?"

I shook my head. "That's Brenda. She's just an employee I

have occasional inappropriate relations with. We have a kind of chemistry. Kind that blows up in a lab."

That got a sultry chuckle out of her.

"Should be dark out, by now," Lu said. "Shall we take care of business?"

I nodded. "No rest for the wicked."

It was dark, all right, nicely so, with the moon glowing behind another overcast sky just enough to provide some context without putting us in the spotlight. We walked by way of the lane to my place, and she stopped at the Mercury station wagon parked along there, using a key she must have got off her late partner's body.

We got in the woodie, with her behind the wheel. She started the engine, then said, "That Chevy out front of your place? Just wheels to dump?"

"Just wheels to dump. My Firebird's in Muskego, waiting for me to sell the Chevy back and collect it."

We were rolling now, nice and easy. "Firebird, huh? Aren't you the wild and crazy guy."

"So they tell me. I'll lead you to the pit."

"Cool."

She pulled in next to the Impala. Her ride, a light blue Camaro, maybe ten years old, was parked there, too. I put the seats down in back of the station wagon, and then we went in and collected the plastic-and-duct-taped bundle, with me taking the feet. We slid him into the back of the woodie and the rear door closing with a *whump* echoed across the lake, like a hunter had just scored a moose.

Soon I was in the Impala, alone with my thoughts, as my headlights cut through a hazy darkness and Lu trailed me in the Mercury wagon, not quite tailgating. My mind was starting to work again. Which meant paranoia was kicking in.

Understand that in my business—the various forms of the killing business I'd indulged in, going all the way back to Vietnam—paranoia is not a bad thing. Paranoia is what keeps you alive. It's caution with an edge. And paranoia had me wondering if I dared take Lu and her word at face value.

We had not yet discussed why Lu—coming onto her presumably longtime partner, about to shoot the man she and he had come to kill—had instead killed that partner. That she had then soothed me, cleaned me up, and resumed a friendly relationship that, let's face it, only lasted a few days in the first place, a lot of years ago.

What was this about?

What was she up to?

My winning personality and bedroom skills did not seem enough to encourage this old female friend of mine to kill for me. So far, I'd just been living the moments—the surprise of having Lu back in my life, the relief that she had chosen to save my ass, the procedure of dealing with a dead body that needed to disappear, even the social time spent together over chili.

No reflection.

Just moments. This moment into the next moment.

Now I was behind the Impala's wheel, chasing my headlights. You might think I'd have felt comfortable, moving through my home turf; but my home turf was a heavily timbered area, a dense dark woods on a night with the moon blotted out by clouds, as I rode a concrete ribbon that I was sharing tonight with nobody but Lu.

That was an exaggeration. We encountered probably four cars on a journey that lasted half an hour and change. But it nonetheless seemed like a desolate, spooky, otherworldly world that I was moving through, as if I were already a ghost.

At the gravel pit, we exchanged cars, and when I started

down the incline toward the drop-off, below which the ice-covered gravel pit waited, I wondered if I was about to be as dead as Simmons. I'd brought along my nine millimeter—it was again in my deep bomber jacket pocket—but what good would it do if she fired her Glock at me just as I rolled out onto the ground from the moving vehicle?

Or she might run me down with the Impala, maybe send it and me over that cliff, jumping to safety herself.

Perhaps it's telling that I didn't consider turning the tables on her to let her take a trip over the edge and into the pit with her partner. Why didn't I? Did I trust her? If so, why?

*What the fuck, Quarry?*

Then I was rolling out of the wagon and it was on its way, then gone, followed by the crunch of the ice giving out, and a gurgling sort of burp from the water below, swallowing it.

Suddenly she was right there, helping me up, both of us in the Impala's headlight glare. She was in a black raincoat, which made a silhouette of her. I brushed the dirt and dust off myself, and answered her facial query—*you all right?*—with a nod.

She drove.

Neither of us said a word on the way back, not once in over half an hour. And then we were both back in the living room of my A-frame, sitting beside each other like kids outside the principal's office, looking at the couple of splotches of blood on the shag carpet that were all that remained of Bruce Simmons.

"I need another shower," I said.

"You got dirty," she allowed. "You do that and I'll clean up the carpet."

"You'll find what you need under the sink," I said, nodding toward the kitchenette.

I shuffled off and took another shower. This time I knew I wasn't still asleep. Wasn't dreaming. I scrubbed and soaped and leaned against the wall letting the needles have me. I came out in a bathrobe and almost bumped into her.

She gazed at me with those almond eyes and I could see that she was beat, too.

"My turn," she said, and moved past me, and took over the bathroom, shutting the door on me. Then the spray was going in there.

Out in the A-frame, she'd done her housekeeping. The area on the shag carpet where the bloodstain and puke had been was moist but clean. The various barricades I'd put together with furniture were disassembled, returned to their places or close enough, and even the bubble-pack under windows was gone, stowed away in the supply room most likely.

"But can she cook?" I said to myself.

I got into some pajama bottoms and went into the guest room, where I regularly slept. I slipped under the sheets and covers, and they felt fine. I'd changed them a few days ago and my routine, going back to the Marines, was to make my bed every day. Hospital corners and all.

She'd had plenty of opportunities to take me out, so I didn't worry about whether it was safe to fall asleep or not. As if I had any choice. A few years ago maybe what I'd been through these past, largely sleepless couple of days and nights wouldn't have fazed me. But I was beat, all right. Dead. Not Simmons dead, but dead enough.

I shut the light off.

"Hey you," she said.

She was framed in the doorway, lights on out there. Tall, leaning against the jamb. A silhouette again, her hair an unruly mane—must have washed it and given it a preliminary towel dry.

I clicked on the nightstand lamp, the glow of which was

yellow—dim but just enough to read by, on nights I couldn't get to sleep.

She had wrapped a towel around her, sarong-style. Dorothy Lamour on the lookout for Bing or Bob. Still in the doorway, she asked, "Interested? Bad timing? Been through a lot, I know. Maybe just sleep?"

Then she dropped the towel.

Fucking beautiful women and what they know they can do to you.

That lanky body with the pendulous breasts, the nipples erect in their dark sand-dollar circles, the lush thatch of dark pubic triangle. The years had only improved her, her legs not so skinny now, her body showing signs of working out. My vivid memory of whiteness left by her bikini when she sunned had been replaced by an all-over tan.

That lovely unusual high-cheekboned face, those almond eyes, the narrow nose, wide mouth, bore no makeup at all. By every stereotypical standard this was not a beautiful woman. But the combination of those features, and the intelligence in those gold-flecked blue orbs, set their own standard of beauty.

Who the hell cared if she could cook?

She came over to me and flipped the covers back. I was erect already.

"Sit," she commanded.

I sat on the edge of the bed and then she was kneeling before me and her head was moving up and down in my lap, the velvety warmth enveloping all of me, not just what her mouth had taken in. Gliding up, gliding down. Her hair was still damp from the shower, its tendrils tickling my thighs as her head gently bobbed, building tempo until she had to stop if she didn't want it to end.

And she didn't.

She guided me onto my back and she climbed on and that sweet receptacle sucked me up into itself. She did all the work, or anyway most of it. Grinding but sweetly, building again, until this time I couldn't hold back and she didn't want me to. We clasped each other, shudderingly, and then she smiled down at me.

"Aren't you glad," she said, "you didn't kill me, all those years ago?"

"Aren't you glad," I said, "you didn't kill me tonight?"

The next morning, around nine, I heard somebody say, "Hey! You! Wake up!"

I got myself in a sitting position, blinked a few times, and there she was, sitting on the edge of the bed, fully dressed—another jumpsuit, but a lemon-color one today—with all her makeup done. She was probably around forty, and the years were showing some, but she knew not to hit the cosmetics too hard and looked just great.

"Question," she said.

"Okay."

"What kind of civilized human doesn't keep any coffee in his house?"

"There's tea. Diet Coke. If caffeine's the point."

She shook her head. No longer in a ponytail, the blondeness got itself nicely tousled. "*Coffee* is the point. Did you have a nice time last night?"

"You mean, dumping that body or getting my ashes hauled?"

"The latter."

"Yeah. I had a nice time."

"Then get up and buy a girl some breakfast."

I narrowed my eyes at her. "Did you move in or something?"

She gestured toward her attire. "Suitcase was in the Camaro.

I don't care how cute a guy is, I don't stay over without toothpaste and a change of clothes."

"You *are* civilized."

After yet another shower, and getting myself into a sweatshirt and jeans, I drove her in the Impala over to Marv's. Today the funky diner-in-an-old-house was busier, but still all locals. Kind of people I didn't know to talk to, just exchange nods with.

We found the same table in the corner I'd taken yesterday, nicely private. Hazel, the skinny waitress with a lot of miles on her, managed to drive herself over and take our order. I had the kitchen sink omelet again and Lu ordered the French toast with bacon, crisp. Hazel, who seemed tickled I was getting a little, had already delivered a fountain version of a Diet Coke to me, and Lu asked for coffee, black.

We didn't talk much while we ate, but when the dishes had been cleared, and the place had emptied out pretty much, I had a refill on the Diet Coke and Lu was having a third cup of coffee, and I finally asked the big question.

"What the fuck," I asked, quiet but firm, "is going on?"

She shrugged, sipped coffee, then jumped right in. "For the last few years, Bruce has been talking about it."

"About what? And don't you call him 'Brace'?"

She shook her head. "No, and he didn't call me 'Ivy,' either. We were a team a long time. You get to know a person."

"Got along?"

"Far as it went. He was kind of an asshole."

"In what way?"

Single shoulder shrug. "Oh, he'd talk about his little family and how much he loved his wife, how crazy he was about her, but then he'd tomcat around on the job. A kid away from home."

"You didn't like that."

"No. First of all, what the hell kind of immoral shit is that?

Second of all, I like working with somebody whose mind stays on the job."

I sipped Diet Coke. "Ever cause you any trouble?"

"Couple times," she admitted. "Twice jobs almost blew up in our faces. Because his eye wasn't on the ball. On *balling*, not the ball."

"I hate that, too. That's what got my partner killed."

She nodded, smirked humorlessly. "Anyway, for a couple of years Bruce had been talking about this rumor that somebody was out there, messing up jobs. Knocking off entire teams, and taking clients down, too."

"Not sure I follow."

Her smile patronized me. "Jack. Please. If that's where we're headed, I'll just kiss you on the cheek for old time's sake and hit the road. You know *exactly* what I mean."

"I do?"

"Sure you do. You're the one who's been doing it."

What could I say to that?

She continued: "You got hold of the Broker's roster, didn't you? How did you put it to use? Follow somebody to a job, figure out who hired it, get paid to make the threat go away? Kind of genius really."

I said nothing.

"I never said anything to Bruce or our middleman for that matter," she went on, "but I figured you were the guy, this ghost who was fucking things up for everybody. Not out of, what…"

"Morality?"

She laughed lightly. "Not out of that. You, what—squeezed dough out of the mark? Using the list to wipe out the hit teams, I see how you might have managed that. But figuring out who *hired* the hits? And taking those bastards out, too? What are you, Magnum P.I.?"

I had some Diet Coke. Then said: "I would guess, if there were anything to this, it would be a matter of working backward. Looking at who had a bullseye on him, and figuring out who was likely to have hung it on."

She shook her head, blondeness bouncing, her half-smile an admiring one. "You know how I figured out it was you, right, Jack? *That* was what you were doing in Des Moines! That was how my cute little partner ended up dead in a bathtub. That was why the plug got pulled on that contract. You've been doing this *that* long?"

Couldn't hold back a little grin. "That was my first time out."

"But why leave me alive?"

"I don't know. The nice tits?"

She'd been sipping coffee and her laugh turned into a snort. She put a napkin to her face, her nose, and when she could talk again, she said, "You might have died yesterday, y'know, if it hadn't been for the way this job went down."

"Oh?"

Hazel came over and filled Lu's coffee and disappeared back behind the counter.

Lu sipped and said, "Our broker, Simmons and mine? We call him the Envoy. Corny as shit I know. Anyway, the Envoy said this job might *look* routine, but it was dangerous as hell, really, and he was doubling our rate."

"What did you make of that?"

"Well, nothing, till I started my surveillance and saw who our mark was." The wide mouth made a wide smile. "You haven't changed much, Jack. You're still a nice-lookin' boy. Clean-cut. Take-you-home-to-meet-mom-and-dad kinda guy."

"Stop. I'll blush."

"The Envoy brought us both in, Simmons and me, and talked to us. That was unusual in itself, because usually he just met with

Simmons, who filled me in after. Not this time. The Envoy warned us both that this time we would be dealing with a very dangerous subject, although, at first glance, the mark…you… might not seem like all that much. Don't be fooled, he said. But what he said *next* was the real eye-opener."

"Yeah?"

"He said, 'The client on this job is yours truly.' The Envoy himself was the fucking client!"

"Why?"

She flipped a hand. "I can only guess. Possibly you've cost him and others in the game a lot of money over the last ten years. So a revenge motive could be part of it."

"Too emotional."

She nodded, smirked. "My feeling exactly. I think it's strictly business. You're a liability out there causing trouble. I mean, you haven't stopped, have you, Jack? You're still working the Broker's list, aren't you?"

I just shrugged.

"Well, I have a list, too," she said lightly.

"Do you now?"

"With just one name. One address."

"Not much of a list."

"Sure it is. It has the Envoy on it."

# EIGHT

Lu and I sat within the kitchenette at the counter with my Rand McNally road atlas open before us, like a menu we were studying.

"Wilmette," she said. "Easy trip. What, an hour fifteen?"

"Hour fifteen," I agreed, adding, "That's one rich suburb. Your Envoy is doing all right for himself."

She smirked. "Wait till you see his digs. Mansion going back to the thirties—not a lot of those got built in Depression days."

"Are you sure," I said, "you can't just show up at his front door and get let in? Loyal employee that you are?"

She shook her head. "*Bruce* was the contact. My coming around unannounced might signal something went wrong, or at least wasn't right. Put his security on red alert."

"How much security is there?"

"No alarm system—anything that would bring the cops around in a crisis is out. But two armed watchdogs are on duty at all times. Four total."

"How'd you come by that morsel?"

With a shrug, she said, "I asked, in passing, on my recent visit. You know, just wondering. Far as the Envoy was concerned."

"He married? Any kids at home?"

"No. Wife dead. Beautiful young thing, but she drowned in a boating accident, on the lake. Lake Michigan."

"Real accident?"

"Oh, hell no. This is not a man who would put up with alimony. Also, word is she cheated on him."

I let out a laugh. "And he's not the kind of man who puts up with cheating."

"Sure he does. His own."

"Describe him."

She looked out toward the lake view, not really seeing it, and thought for a while. "About your height. Five ten?"

"Five ten," I said.

"About fifty, fifty-five. Bald on top, gray on the sides. Narrow face. Friendly features except for the dead eyes. Slim. Dresses well, even at home. Golfer. Country club all the way."

"You know the latter how? More 'just wondering'?"

She shook her head. "I was ushered into his home office when Bruce and I got the assignment. You know—the one to kill you?"

"Oh, that assignment."

"He had pictures on the wall, some with local and state politicians, most on the golf course. Various award plaques and framed certificates, including one citing him as country-club president, five years ago. His straight business is real estate."

"Nice eye for detail, lady. He dangerous?"

Lu shook her head. "Not physically. The security guys are. Referrals from Chicago associates. Badass ex-military types."

"Ever more than two on duty at a time, you think?"

"Can't be sure, but probably just two."

"We handle them how?"

She shrugged. "We fucking kill them. And when we're done with the Envoy—whose name is Charles Vanhorn, by the way—we won't leave *him* breathing, either. Does all this carnage disturb your delicate sensibilities?"

I shook my head. "No, but three dead in a rich suburb. Including a mobbed-up homeowner? Lots of different kinds of people will be looking for us."

She nodded slowly. "Other alternatives?"

I placed a hand on her sleeve. "Only one. You in shape for a disappearing act? Got enough put away for that? Willing to walk off from that antiques business in St. Paul? Ready to retire, maybe, with the kind of nice boy you could take home to mom and dad, as long as first he washed the blood and brains off his face?"

She didn't say anything for a while.

"We both aren't getting any younger," she noted.

"Nobody is." I was too genteel to point out she was a good five years older than me.

"And I'm not sure," she said, "we can just walk away and take on new lives, new identities, no matter *how* well we're fixed." She squinted at me appraisingly. "You could *afford* to quit?"

I opened a hand. "Yes, but do I have a choice? I haven't filled a contract in ten years. And my cottage industry, working off the Broker's list, seems to be common knowledge now, in certain circles."

She nodded. "Good point. But we don't know yet whether Vanhorn has talked about you or not, and what you've been up to, to others like him. Which is to say, middlemen in the murder business."

Now I was nodding. "We'd have to find that out. Which is probably reason enough for a Wilmette trek."

"Probably is," she said. "And if it turns out you're on the radar of every murder broker in the country—and, through them, the mob families they're linked with—you may need a desert island, plastic surgery and a prayer."

"Not a wonderful option."

She let out a big sigh. "Only other one I can think of is Witness Protection. You *might* know enough about organized crime to worm your way into WITSEC."

I didn't love that alternative, and anyway my knowledge was fairly limited on that score. Working with an agent of sorts was designed to keep information about clients at a minimum. And, anyway, I'd only done a handful of gigs that were outright mob hits.

"If," I said, "Vanhorn has kept what he knows to himself, I might be able to contain this thing. Will he talk, with a gun in his face?"

The almond eyes narrowed. "I'd say so. He *thinks* he's a bad man, but he's soft. Like the Broker was soft, and all of these businessmen who traffic in crime and murder are soft, all tucked away in their secure little respectable lives."

I frowned. "I'm not into torture. I saw too much of that overseas. Distasteful shit."

"I can handle that," she said with a shrug. "I'll just clip his toenails."

"*That'll* make him talk?"

"If I start at the toe knuckle it will."

That was worth a chuckle. "Okay. After dark?"

"*Way* after dark. Before we leave, I can phone in and tell Vanhorn you've been taken care of, which'll let us know if he's home."

I squinted at her. "Won't he be expecting to hear from your partner, not you?"

She shrugged. "I'll just say Bruce is busy getting rid of…you know."

"My earthly remains. Yeah. Still…that *is* an opportunity to arrange a meet. To get in the front door."

"Not our best option. You can't exactly show up with me…"

"Being dead and all."

"…and his security boys would be on their toes, making it tricky to sneak you in. I think we're better off throwing a surprise party."

"And me without a party hat."

"Your noisemaker will do."

I smiled, then frowned. "You were only in that house the once?"

"Like I said, Bruce usually took the meets."

"Did you pay attention?"

She made a face. "No, I just sat there and let my mind wander. *Of course* I paid attention. Get me a sheet of paper and a pencil or something, and I'll sketch the layout."

I frowned. "How much did you see of the place on your one visit?"

"Everything." Another shrug. "I excused myself to use the restroom and had a quick look around, upstairs and down. Even saw the security boys in their little quarters. They were watching a soap opera. Kinda sweet, isn't it?"

"Sweet as shit. Why such foresight, Lu?"

"Jack, how *did* you stay alive so long?" She yawned, stretched. "I always check the exits, wherever I am. Not everybody in this business is as nice as we are."

Lu drew the layout of the Vanhorn manse, both floors, and also a crude but useful little map of the streets of the suburban subdivision, with the house in question at the end of a cul-de-sac. I was pleased to learn that no homes were close on either side.

We studied her handiwork and discussed different approaches of entry. The biggest problem, it seemed to her, was the security guards, and she wasn't wrong. One or both guards might be expected to make rounds outside, and she had no idea what that schedule might be.

Around one PM we drove back over to Twin Lakes and returned to Marv's diner—this time of year our options were limited—and had cheeseburgers and fries and even shared a malt. I played the jukebox, which had some '50s tunes on it.

When I returned to our table in the corner, she was sitting there in her lemon jumpsuit sipping on her straw on her half of the malt. She looked up at me with those gold-flecked blue eyes and said, "Look at us. Couple of kids down at Pop's soda shop, listening to the devil's music."

"Where's your poodle skirt?"

She smiled and her gums showed. "I did have one, you know. Did you ever have a pompadour?"

I shook my head. "Just missed that era. I had a soup bowl haircut I thought made me look like John Lennon. My mother said more like Moe Howard. My father said I reminded him of Ish Kabibble. I never knew who that was till Turner started showing old movies."

She squinted at me, maybe imagining the haircut. "He was a cornet player, wasn't he? With Kay Kyser's Kollege of Musical Knowledge?"

"You *are* older than me."

She slapped my hand. "Be nice." She sipped more malt. "Or we could just disappear."

"What?"

"You round up your money, I'll round up mine, and we just go south of the border." She sang softly, "Meh-hi-co way."

Marty Robbins was singing "El Paso." Not quite down Mexico way, but close.

"That body will turn up," I said. "The Chicago glee club will see your partner dead and me gone and you nowhere, and put two and two together, or maybe three and three, and..."

"Come looking." She nodded over her straw. "I know. How did we get here?"

She wasn't talking about geography.

I said, "I don't know."

"I had a normal life. Regular childhood."

"Me, too."

"But events conspired."

"They'll do that."

Those almond eyes looked moist.

"You okay?" I asked.

She leaned in. "We should've stopped this shit ten years ago. We could have, you know. If we'd just disappeared then, who would have cared?"

"But we didn't." I shrugged. "Maybe this is a second chance."

"Maybe. But we're going to have to kill some people."

I shrugged again. "I'm okay with that."

She shrugged. Sipped. "So am I. You'll have to excuse me, Jack. I'm just a sentimental slob sometimes."

Elvis was singing.

*It's Now Or Never.*

I had it in my head she was some kind of superwoman. She certainly had rolled with the punches better than I had, over these past less-than-twenty-four hours of madness.

But she was human, too, and she stripped out of her pantsuit and left on the pop-arty orange bra and panties beneath and climbed into my bed and was asleep faster than I could get out of the bomber jacket.

So I left it on. I wrote a note and set it on the kitchenette counter, in case she woke up before I got back. Didn't think she would, because she was snoring, really sawing logs.

Made me smile. I liked that she was human. Kind of a nice side benefit.

I got in the Impala and drove over to Wilma's and pulled in at a pump. Filled the tank, then parked in the small front lot before walking around to the side of the building and up the steps and inside.

The register was unattended—Brenda wasn't on just yet—but the bar was open. No customers right now, just Charley sitting on a stool behind the counter reading the *Lake Geneva News*. On the puss of the old hard-ass, that neutral expression seemed like a glare.

He lowered the paper. "Diet Coke, Jack?"

"Please."

When he delivered the soda, I said, "I'll be away for a while."

"One of your lengthy sojourns?"

"Probably not. But at least one night. Maybe longer."

"Why do you bother with it? Your sideline."

"Huh?"

His shrug was elaborate. "We make decent money here, Jack. Why fuck with them veterinary drugs, anyhow? You ain't out and about enough to make much offa that."

"I told you before. I have people working for me, but now and then a client wants to talk to the boss. That so hard for you to imagine, Charley, somebody who wants to talk to his boss?"

He shrugged. "To each his own."

"Look, if, uh...you still have that envelope salted away, right?"

"Sure."

Though no one was around, I kept my voice down. "If I'm not back in a week, or you haven't heard from me by phone? You know where to get that envelope to. Right?"

He nodded. "Sure. Do I look like an idiot?"

Was that a trick question?

"I just need to know," I said, "you'll take care of it. If necessary."

"Jesus, we go through this every time, Jack! You drop off the edge of the earth, I'm to open the envelope. There's an address in it and a, what-do-you-call-it."

"A document."

He nodded a bunch of times. "Document, right."

"Go back to your paper, Charley."

"You pissed at me or something?"

"No. I just remember when a bartender was like a friendly priest you could go to. Or a marriage counselor."

The rumpled face formed a smirk. "You ain't married *or* Catholic."

I worked on the Diet Coke.

The document was my will. It wasn't detailed, and I hadn't used a lawyer. It merely stated that my worldly goods, including Wilma's Welcome Inn, were to go to my father in Ohio. He was my only living relative, and we hadn't spoken for years. Far as he was concerned, most likely, I was already dead.

It's just that if I died without a will—intestate they called it—the authorities would start in snooping.

And for some fucking reason I couldn't explain to you, the idea that my life would be poked around in after my death, in a way that exposed all the killing, well…I just didn't like the idea. The media would get hold of it and make me into a monster. I'd be Charles Manson or Ted Bundy or something, and that wouldn't be fair.

I don't mean fair to me—when you're dead, fairness isn't an issue.

But it wouldn't be fair to my father, or the occasional decent people I'd encountered in my lifetime. Including some women I'd loved or very nearly so.

Which is why, if you're wondering, I have written these accounts. I understand they don't always present me in the best light. But they are honest. They're the truth. And it's a way to let you know that I wasn't just some psycho killer.

I was heading out and almost bumped into Brenda, coming

in. She was in her work togs—white blouse and black skirt—and her big feathered brown hair framed her pretty features nicely, the bruised red mouth jumping at me.

"Well, Jack," she said, blocking the way. "Where's your hooker gone to?"

"She's not a hooker, Brenda. She's an old friend."

"Old is right." She brushed by me and got behind the counter and took her position at the register. "Sometimes I think you're too dumb to know when you already have a good thing going."

I leaned on the counter. "That would be you, right? The good thing?"

Her head cocked, her mouth tightened. She let some words out. "You really want to risk our relationship over some dried-up prune?"

I laughed. "Relationship? Really?"

"I could go to a lawyer, you know. Sexual harassment, it's called."

"Right. Brenda, I'm going to be gone for a day or two, maybe a little longer. I need you to keep an eye on things."

"Going off with your ancient hooker, are you?"

"Never mind where I'm going. Just do your job. If I'm not back for payday, Charley will take care of you."

She touched my hand. "Let's go upstairs. This register isn't open yet. I'll remind you what you have going."

Was her ego really insulted, or was she just trying to hang onto her access to the register?

"Honey," I said, no acid at all, "I really am going to be gone on business. Just look after things. We'll have a good time when I get back."

"You know, Jack," she said, eyes big, "I really do like you. I usually don't like the men I'm with."

"You're sweet," I somehow managed to say.

Lu was still asleep when I got back. I nestled next to her and, when I woke, the windows were full of night and Lu was up, getting into yet another jumpsuit. A black one this time, suitable for the commando mission we'd be mounting.

I got into a black sweatshirt and black jeans and black sneakers. A fleece-lined black leather jacket—not motorcycle style, but with a custom pocket like the bomber jacket—would complete the ensemble.

Well, almost.

I dropped the noise-suppressed nine mil in the custom jacket pocket, a .38 snubnose in the other pocket, and had Lu duct-tape a switchblade along my spine above the belt line.

"Road trip?" Lu asked with a smile.

"Road trip," I said.

# NINE

I found myself on Highway 12 again, rural landscape alternating with urban spread till the latter took over. Traffic was neither light nor heavy, as we'd started out around ten PM, making the trip to Wilmette in the predicted hour and fifteen. Reaching Indian Hills Estates, however—north of Lake Street and west of Illinois Road—took another twenty minutes.

We were in my temporary ride, the Impala, which seemed less attention-getting then Lu's Camaro; nonetheless, she drove, having been to the Envoy's home before. We said little on the way. We didn't have the radio on, not even Easy Listening. When you're getting ready to invade a home, particularly one with a couple of armed guards on the loose, getting mentally prepared is a must.

We glided between the stone markers of what had once been farmland but was now a subdivision, a couple hundred acres of big honking houses, winding roads, yawning front yards and wooded areas. Right now all the trees were still winter bare, but for the occasional stubborn snow clinging to branches. Spring would thicken up these barriers, make them nice and green and plush; but this time of year we had minimal cover.

"Money," I said, taking it all in as we rolled through the neighborhood.

"Money," she said with a nod. She was in the ponytail again, and it bounced.

The houses perched on endless lots, with no set style—Colonials, Tudors, Arts and Craft, even ranch-styles. Some homes had been here a good while, others showing signs of recent construction. Apparently some smaller homes, dating way back, were going down to make room for big new ones.

The Vanhorn place seemed here to stay, however, an English Manor-style shades-of-tan brick-and-stone affair with dark brown shutters, a two-car garage, two peaked roofs each with a chimney, and a yard no larger than Versailles.

We parked on the next street over in front of a chain-link fenced-off lot with a sign that said DEMOLITION/NEW CONSTRUCTION SITE. No one likely to complain about us leaving the Impala here. Across the street was a Colonial with a FOR SALE sign and no signs of life. That was also good.

The houses were far enough apart to make it unlikely that anyone would notice us strolling across and into the trees. We were soon moving through the park-like area of the adjoining back yards of the mansions, demarcated only by low-riding shrubbery. Lu led the way and I walked backward, right behind her. Our tight-gloved right hands held our noise-suppressed automatics along our sides as we quick-stepped across. The night was cold but not windy.

Vanhorn's back yard was landscaped only at its edges, the expansive rest of it open, its winter-brown grass painted ivory in the cloud-filtered moonlight, almost blending in with a gray stone patio with outdoor fireplace, wrought-iron furniture and enough room for the Marine Corps Band to rehearse. The back door would let us into a finished basement, specifically a recreation room visible through windows and the windowed back door, whose Yale deadbolt I opened in a couple minutes with two picks.

Lu had been right about the lack of an electronic security system—or least one that set off a noisy alarm. And I figured she was right that a silent alarm that brought the cops was unlikely. The two security guards on duty were the only threat that faced us.

No sign of them yet.

We both had mini-flashlights in our pockets, but neither of us had them out as we stepped inside, where track lighting had been left on, on this lower level, at a dim but serviceable setting.

The ample rec room was decked out with a treadmill and other exercise equipment, a green-felt poker table, black-leather couch and comfy chairs, a big projection TV, and off-white walls arrayed with framed Chicago Bears and Cubs memorabilia.

Batwing doors opened into a spacious, appliance-filled laundry room where stairs led up into a vast kitchen also decked out with the latest appliances, and enough seating at an island for that Marine band on break. Though the house was Depression-era, this kitchen and the rooms beyond were all renovated into bland modernity, though the furnishings within the white-trimmed walls (pale shades of ash, peach, lime, mauve) were lush dark wood and overstuffed dark-brown leather.

Still no sign of the security guys. They hadn't been outside. When we'd peeked into the two-car garage, off the kitchen, two vehicles were parked there, a Mercedes and a tricked-out Jeep. So somebody was home. But the first floor seemed spookily quiet—just the hum of kitchen appliances and the ticking, and occasional chiming, of clocks.

Our flashlights never came out of our pockets. Lights were on here and there, table lamps, dimmed track lighting. Easy enough to get around in, but with an eerie feel. It was like walking through a haunted house and then realizing you were the ghost.

We had prearranged that Lu would go upstairs and check things out, and bring Vanhorn down at gunpoint if he was already in bed. Meanwhile I checked on a room toward the back of the place, where the security guards hung out.

Lu's sketch had indicated a couple of single beds, a couch, a card table and a TV. Her memory proved accurate enough, but a surprise was still waiting for me, and I hadn't spotted it at first, as it was off to my left as I came in.

A guy was in there—all in black, not unlike the way I was dressed. Sturdy-looking individual with short hair befitting the ex-military man he almost certainly was. Muscular and mean-looking, he'd have made a formidable opponent.

If he wasn't dead.

He lay on his back, and his eyes were open and staring, and it seemed like the hole in his forehead was doing the same. Resting on a pillow of gore he'd produced, he had a peaceful expression, like he hadn't even had time to say, "Oh, shit!" Or even think it.

I heard something behind me, spun, and it was Lu.

"Good way to get killed," I whispered.

She was frowning down at the dead man. "Did you do this?"

"Not that I recall." I knelt, checked him out. "Rigor. Been dead a while."

That made it unlikely the killer, or killers, were still around. Rigor took at least four hours to set in.

She kept her voice down anyway. "Vanhorn's not upstairs. Nobody is. Let's check out the den."

That was on the first floor, too, off the living room, with which it shared the only wood paneling in the place, and I'm not talking about the stuff in your uncle's den where he hangs his beer neons—I mean the rich, dark-brown burnished wood of wealth that goes well with overstuffed leather furnishings.

We lingered in the living room, not to enjoy the stone fireplace, in which a fire would have been nice on a cold night, nor to admire the Oriental carpet that must have been worth a small fortune. I hoped the carpet wouldn't be ruined by that dead man sprawled on it, with his brains spilled out in clumps caught in now-congealed blood like inappropriate vegetables in your grandmother's Jell-O-mold delight.

This was another ex-soldier badass, now not nearly the threat he would once have been. In black, like his dead cohort and me (and Lu for that matter), he too was in a state of rigor mortis. Both watchdogs had died some time ago, but not long ago enough for the rigor to give way.

Lu whispered, though neither of us was sure why. "What do you make of this?"

"Somebody killed them."

That made her smile. Gotta love a girl with a sense of humor.

She said, "I have a hunch our host won't have much to say for himself."

"Me, too. He's either lammed or gone to the Happy Hunting Ground with his two braves."

She had no argument with that assessment.

The living room had been substantial. The den, however, was small for this cathedral of capitalism. It was a book room with no built-in bookshelves, its windowless walls lined with more leather-cushioned furnishings and decorated with those framed photos of Chicago political figures that Lu had reported. Also, hanging perfectly straight, were some pics taken of professional golfers and celebrities at Vanhorn's country club, posing with him.

The desk was a massive mahogany cube, the slab-like top of which indicated a man who wanted everything in its place—folders, papers, pen holder, reference books. A neat freak, this guy. Kind of ironic that he had wound up on the floor near his perfect work area, in a tailored suit and a red-and-blue striped silk tie, in a rumpled sprawl of brains and blood, his mouth open, tongue lolling, eyes wide with as much expression as billiard balls.

"I'm gonna take a leap," I said, "and say this fucker is dead."

"What the hell, Jack? You're *sure* you didn't do this?"

"No, I sneaked out while you thought I was sleeping, drove over here using the drawings you made of this place, and wiped everybody out like the goddamn plague. Why don't you tell me what *you* think happened here? Who *you* think did this?"

"No fucking clue," she said. She was shaking her head. Said, "No fucking clue" again and sat on a couch under framed photos of the bald man on the floor back when he was alive, with Bob Hope and Arnold Palmer smiling next to him, each with an arm around his shoulders.

I paced. This little home office, overwhelmed by the king-size desk, was just large enough for that. "Could this have nothing to do with me?"

She shrugged. "I suppose. A guy like the Envoy would have enemies."

I stopped. "Don't call him the Envoy. It's stupid. He's not the Joker and he's not the Penguin. He's a mobbed-up prick named Vanhorn. A *dead* mobbed-up prick named Vanhorn. And he was waiting to get a phone call from your pal Simmons about *me* being dead."

"So?"

"So?" I stopped in front of her where she sat, as she looked up blandly at me. "Are you kidding? What's been happening lately in the life of Charles Vanhorn, respectable Chicagoland citizen?"

"What?"

"Jesus, Lu, just that he found out some asshole called Quarry has spent the last ten years killing people whose agent he's been, an annoying asshole who has taken real money out of his pocket, and the pockets of other middlemen in murder like him. For ten years!"

She stood. Her tone was firm. No nonsense. "We should go. It's a house with three murdered criminals in it, Jack. Get ahold of yourself. *We should go.*"

"Not just yet. You sit back down. I can handle this."

Her eyes got big. "Handle what?"

"I don't know exactly."

I went over and started looking through things on that fussily neat desktop, standing on the visitor side, facing the dead man's empty black leather-cushioned swivel chair, as if it were supervising me. Though my gloves fit snug, it was kind of awkward. A notepad was perfectly positioned in front of his telephone. The note paper on top had something written on it.

Neatly, almost prissily inscribed, one above the other, were four names. But then, scrawled at an angle alongside, a note: "*Attend sem.*"

I asked Lu, "Any of these names ring any bells? George Callen?"

She shook her head.

"Henry Poole?"

She shook her head.

"Alex Kraft?"

She shook her head.

"Joseph Field?"

She shook her head.

"Might mean something," I said, shrugged, and pocketed the slip of paper. "Might not. Might be guys he goes golfing with."

"Not this time of year," she said, crossing her legs as she sat there, bored in my presence and that of the stiff on the floor. "Unless he was heading south, or *somewhere* warm, anyway."

"He may have gone someplace real warm."

I poked around some more and came up with an address book. A fairly sparse listing of contacts gave up phone numbers and addresses. These may well have been golfing pals, and others in respectable Wilmette circles. Some numbers lacked area codes, indicating locals. A few had area codes elsewhere in Illinois.

The final page, however, had four disparate area codes attached to four names, phone numbers only, no addresses. Only four names at all on the page. You probably already know what they were: *George Callen, Henry Poole, Alex Kraft, Joseph Field.*

"Now," I said, looking down at the notebook, "isn't that interesting?"

Suddenly Lu was up and off the couch and looking over my shoulder. She was tall enough to do that. I glanced back at her and the almond-shaped eyes were slivers.

She asked, "The other brokers?"

"Maybe." I ripped the page out, folded and pocketed it. "We'll look up the area codes later. For now let's keep at it."

We got behind the desk. She worked on going through the drawers and I went through mail in his IN AND OUT box. Nothing seemed significant, no bills or bank statements—mostly charities he was generously supporting to keep people from realizing he was a no good rat bastard who dealt in other's people's deaths.

Then a color brochure jumped out at me.

I knew the location at once—the pictures were of the Lake Geneva Golf and Ski Resort. And while the colorful shots were indeed of the lodge in its summer months, when golfing ruled, I knew a golfing trip to my back yard had not been why

Charles Vanhorn—yes, the fucking Envoy—had kept this on his desk.

Or was he just planning ahead, for a getaway weekend a few months from now?

I tried to take that notion seriously. Tried to make this just an odd coincidence, when the invitation slipped out. Of heavier stock, with genuine engraving, it said:

*Charles Vanhorn*
*is cordially invited*
*to a Seminar*
*by distinguished investment guru*
*Seymour M. Goldman—*
*"The Cayman Islands Plan"*
*Lake Geneva Golf and Ski Resort,*
*Lake Geneva, Wisconsin*

The date below was this weekend, coming up.

I showed it to her and asked, "What do you make of that?"

"That's not far from you," she said, frowning, "is it?"

I admitted it. Then I said, "If these four names are Vanhorn's fellow brokers…maybe *I'm* on the agenda of this seminar."

"You could be, I suppose," she said, eyes tight with thought. "But if they *are* Vanhorn's peers, they're ripe for the kind of offshore banking opportunities this seminar is about. So maybe it's just a…"

"Coincidence? Right. Like the three dead assholes in this mausoleum are a coincidence."

"We need to get out of here, Jack."

"Maybe we should try to find a wall safe in here somewhere? Vanhorn's list of hired guns is supposed to be in it."

She smiled. "Why, Jack? Do you have safe-cracking prowess?"

"No. Do you?"

"No. We need to get *out* of here, Jack!"

We got out.

Got out the way we came, and then we were heading back to Wisconsin, the traffic even lighter now. This time I drove. We didn't talk for the first ten or fifteen minutes, each sorting out this lunacy in the privacy of our own minds.

Finally I said, "Who wanted Vanhorn dead?"

"Could be a lot of people." She shrugged. "Business he was in, ties he had. Could have been anything or anybody from that world."

I shot a glance at her. "But it happened now, on the heels of him sending you and Simmons to cap my ass. What the hell, Lu? Would one of Vanhorn's 'peers,' as you put it, want to take him out, to take over his business?"

"Possible," she said. "If he had told the others about you, and what you've been up to, that might make somebody want to consolidate and take over and do things right. I mean, you got away with offering your particular…service, shall we say… for a damn decade. Much of it at Vanhorn's expense, since most of the Broker's people went over to him."

"But all four of the seminar attendees took it in the teeth because of me, too, at one point or another. Not often enough to see a pattern maybe, but…."

The almond eyes got as wide as they could. "Right. But that gets *you* killed, not Vanhorn. Any ideas?"

"Oh, well, sure. I don't know about you, but I'm going to that seminar."

I was wrong about those eyes—they *could* get bigger.

"You can't be serious," she said. "If they *do* know about you…."

I grinned and it probably looked a little crazy. "They may know *about* me, but they don't *know* me. They don't know what I look like."

"You can't be sure of that."

"I'm sure enough. I have two choices, Lu. I pack up my marbles and go running off to God knows where, to what? Find a new game? Hide out for the rest of my life? Or I can take in the seminar. Come with me. Don't you want to know where to stow your ill-gotten gains?"

# TEN

When Lu, in my pajama top, stumbled into the A-frame living room from out of the bedroom down the hall, I was in the kitchenette making scrambled eggs and bacon. In my pajama bottoms and a t-shirt and bare feet. No chef's hat.

Her blondeness was nicely tousled and the Asian eyes were still sleepy. "And he cooks."

"I can do breakfast, passably. No coffee, but there's tea. Also, refrigerator biscuits and, later, all manner of frozen dinners. Sit down."

She climbed onto one of the chairs—really stools with high backs—on the other side of the counter. I served her up, and myself, then sat opposite her. She began slowly, poking at the food, but soon picked up her pace. We didn't talk. We hadn't talked much last night, either, on the rest of the ride back or on our return around two-thirty AM, when we just crawled into bed together.

I gathered the dishes and went over to dump them in the sink and run some water over them while she sipped at her second cup of tea. I, of course, had a can of Diet Coke going, as do all civilized people at breakfast.

She asked, "Did I dream that?"

I returned to my seat. "Which part?"

"The three dead guys I accept as reality. You thinking we should crash that Cayman Islands party…I can't really have *heard* that, right?"

I swigged Diet Coke. "I have a satellite dish."

She just looked at me. Did not blink, just looked. My apparent non-sequitur would have been hard for anybody to respond to, let alone someone who just got up.

"Good for you," she managed.

"I was up a couple of hours ago and watched the Chicago news. It's on the satellite because WGN is part of most basic cable."

"How interesting."

"How interesting is this? Seems a prominent Wilmette business leader was murdered. Also, two of his security people. Police discovered this after the security shift changed early this morning. Apparent a home invasion gotten out of hand. It's early stages of the investigation, obviously, so nothing else is known. Or anyway nothing else was shared."

"That was quick," she said, one eyebrow arching.

"Not really. We could have anticipated Vanhorn and his guards would be found when the other two guards came on shift. I thought maybe, with Vanhorn's connections, there'd have been some kind of cover-up, or stall, before the media got it. You know, till the place had been swept of anything incriminating as to any mob ties of his. Otherwise, I pretty much expected this."

She leaned her elbows on the counter and her palms pressed against her cheeks and what was showing of her face stared at me. "This shows you, doesn't it?"

"Shows me what?"

"That we can't…infiltrate that seminar. I never really thought we could, but surely now you can see…"

"That we *have* to? Or anyway I have to. Optional, in your case. But I'd remind you that your precious Envoy was murdered, while you were off supposedly helping murder me. And that my cottage industry of interfering in mob-sanctioned murder has been exposed—on some level, anyway. So I have to get, uh…what's that stupid word everybody's using lately? Proactive."

She shrugged, then—her voice very quiet—said, "I don't. Have to. Be proactive."

Now I just looked at her. "I cooked you breakfast," I reminded her.

She smiled just a little. "Yes, but no coffee. I'm looking for a man who can make me breakfast *with* coffee."

"I'm willing to work on that." I gave her half a smile in return. "Look, I can't tell you exactly how this impacts your life, or even your work. Maybe it doesn't. You can probably go back to St. Paul and sell antiques for now. Then if some new broker or envoy shows up and wants to represent your considerable talents, hey, groovy. But right now? I could use your help."

More tea. "Accompanying you to that seminar."

I nodded. "One of those 'peers' of Vanhorn's killed him—that's all but certain. We have four of them—the likely four I'll bet—all in one place, just a few miles from here. Which provides the opportunity to sort things out and find out where we stand."

She was leaning back now. "By 'sort things out,' you mean kill whoever's responsible."

"The way you say it makes it sound a little harsh."

That got a bigger smile out of her. "What do you want out of this, Jack?" Her tone turned arch. "Surely not to be able to start using the list again, to hit hitters and save the scum they were hired to remove."

I shook my head. "No, that ship has sailed. But I'm well-off enough, and have a successful enough straight business here, to want to find a way *not* to have to run."

"I get that."

"But even if I *do*, first I'd like to tie off as many loose ends as possible."

"Which is better than being a loose end yourself."

"Much. And that might be how you'd wind up, Lu—a loose end. To be fair, though, with your skills, whoever the new Envoy, the new Broker, might turn out to be…you would probably be viewed a valuable asset."

Her forehead frowned but her mouth smiled. "Are you trying to talk me out of it now, Jack? Out of helping you?"

"No, honey. I'm genuinely fond of you. And I owe you. You saved my life the other day. True, you blew the guy's brains out right in my face, which was a little gross…"

That made her laugh. I told you, great sense of humor on the girl.

"…but if you want to quit," I went on, "whether to focus on antiques or run off and start over at something else that *isn't* murder for hire…well, even the best pro athletes know their careers can't go on forever."

"And I'm getting older."

"So am I. Not as old as you, of course."

She grinned, gums showing, and slapped my arm.

Then her grin softened into just a small smile. Very quietly she said, "You're right, Jack. I am looking for the exit out of this game. I have a successful front business, too, with enough stashed away to leave this risky, dangerous life behind. But starting over with all these…yes, loose ends dangling, I'd be looking over my shoulder all day and afraid to go to sleep at night."

I touched her hand. "With everything you know," I said, "walking away? You would stop being an asset and move into the liability column. Me—now that what I've been up to for the last decade has been exposed—I don't have any choice, really. I *have* to figure out what's going on, and do something about it."

Her nodding was barely perceptible, then she said, "I know this seminar thing is almost literally in your back yard…but how does that not make matters worse? You're *known* around here. The smalltime owner of Wilma's Welcome Inn wants to attend a seminar about hiding bigtime money in the Cayman Islands? Are you kidding?"

I gestured vaguely toward the north. "That resort in Lake Geneva, where it's being held? The manager of the place is a friend of mine. He's in my monthly poker game—has been in this very room many times, losing small stakes to me. I can talk to him. He can help me make this happen."

"You think so?"

"I do. I'll sit down with him and get the logistics worked out. If I can't get his help, his cooperation, I'll spike the whole fucking idea." I gave her what I hoped was my most winning smile. "Wouldn't you like a couple of days at an exclusive resort? I'm buying."

She laughed again. "Okay. Talk to your friend. If you can make this fly..."

"You'll be my co-pilot?"

"Thanks for not saying 'stewardess.' "

"It's 'flight attendant' now. Aren't you keeping up with the feminist newsletters? So. Are you on board?"

Her sigh was half laugh. "Yeah. Just don't expect me to say 'Reporting for duty, Captain.' "

"Deal. Coffee, tea or me? But we're out of coffee."

Three miles beyond Lake Geneva was what had been, until a few years ago, the Playboy Club Hotel, a striking, sprawling architectural anomaly flung across the Wisconsin countryside. This wood-and-stone geometric tribute to Frank Lloyd Wright-style modernism had attracted, over the years, tens of thousands of guests—couples in particular taking advantage of the seven attached buildings, two championship golf courses, indoor and outdoor swimming pools (connecting), and a ski lounge shaped like two interlaced snowflakes.

The drive from my A-frame to what was now the Lake Geneva

Golf and Ski Resort took not quite half an hour. I was still in the Impala, but on my own, Lu waiting back home to see what I'd be able to pull off with the manager here, my poker buddy Dan Clark. And I admit to having reservations, though not at the lodge.

Not yet.

The parking lot was almost empty, probably not at all surprising in mid-afternoon, when I'd arranged to meet with Dan. This time of year was a dead one for the resort, which was the case even in better days, back when you never knew whether Hef might not drop by with Barbi Benton on his arm. The good old days, when the beautiful cotton-tailed, rabbit-eared waitresses lived on site in the Bunny Dorm.

What had been a big deal, back in May '68 when it opened as the first Playboy Club Hotel, now seemed vaguely shabby and something of a relic—yesterday's hip becoming today's kitsch. Two of the three restaurant/bars had closed, including the disco and assorted shops as well as the barbershop and beauty salon. The nightclub where I'd seen performers like Peggy Lee, Tony Bennett, Liza Minnelli, and Sonny and Cher was now only a dining room. And the three-hundred-and-fifty guest rooms in the Main Lodge were rarely filled, even at the height of the summer and winter seasons.

When the resort shuttered in the early '80s, the Chicago media had cited "changing tastes and poor financial performance." What had been exciting a few decades ago, against a backdrop of the opening guns of the sexual revolution, seemed suddenly absurd and misjudged next to the casualties of the AIDS epidemic.

But when I strolled through the lobby, half-expecting tumbleweed to blow through, the Playboy trappings were still very much in evidence—the sunken lounge, the glass-encased fireplace, the pebbled walls, and a rain forest of tropical plants, the latter looking admittedly a little wilted.

No bunnies to frolic through, either—just one young woman behind the optimistically long check-in counter, her nice figure ensconced in a white blouse with a colorful scarf at her neck that would not require her to learn the serving technique known as the Bunny dip.

I joined Dan Clark in a button-tufted booth on the elevated outer level of a bar about as underpopulated as the one at Wilma's right now. What had been the Playmate Bar, decorated by framed fold-outs of fetching fillies (sorry), was just a bar, stripped of its bosoms on display with only tacky burgundy carpet and a lot of dark wood left behind, as clues to better times.

Dan half-stood while I slid in, flashing a grin that had a sideways tilt that always made you feel like you and he were in on some private joke. At forty or so, he was one of those guys whose slenderness and narrow, angular features made him seem tall, when he was really only a few inches taller than I was.

"You're going to insult me," he said, effortlessly handsome, his hair dark and short, his eyes dark and sharp, "if you just order a Diet Coke. This is a bar. Where alcoholic beverages are served. Try to be a man, Jack."

"I'll give it a go."

And when a pretty blonde waitress, in white shirt, colorful scarf and black slacks, took my order, I made it Diet Coke and Bacardi. When in Rome. Even if the orgy was over.

As you might expect, I was in a long-sleeve t-shirt and black jeans, but my friend was in a sharp tailored suit, mocha brown, with a narrow silk tie, striped shades of brown.

"That's a nice suit, Dan. Sears or Ward's?"

"Pucci of Chicago."

"Tie was for Christmas? Your Aunt Clara?"

"Pierre Cardin."

"Thoughtful of Pierre. Didn't know you two exchanged, at Christmas."

"Are you here for the janitorial job, Jack? If I'd known, I'd have brought an application form."

We were friends. We gave each other shit.

Nodding around us, I said, "We're not doing much business, either, Dan. At Wilma's."

"Give me time," he said, glancing around at the big, mostly empty room. A few businessmen were at the bar, but that was about it. "I'm only a year in. My contract guarantees five."

I gestured with an open hand. "Listen, I love this place. Many happy times here. But I don't have to tell you it's not what it was."

He smirked. Bastard even smirked handsomely.

"I know, Jack. Before my time, but back then this place was *it*. You could fly here directly from O'Hare and back again, you know."

I did know—the resort had once had a private airstrip.

He went on: "But in those days, this place was all about couples. I know we have to go another way now—need to attract *families*, and with the swimming pools and ski lifts and golf and everything, that'll be a snap. Kids welcome!"

"Somewhere Hefner is weeping."

Dan shrugged. "It's not his property anymore, Jack. You know where else the money is these days? The meeting market."

"Yeah, the meat market. Picking up babes at last call. Never grows old."

He ignored the lame joke. "That's the first thing I did, you know."

"Pick a babe up at last call?"

"No, man. Break ground on our retreat chalet."

Our drinks arrived. He was drinking bourbon on the rocks, or least something amber brown with ice in it. I sipped my rum and Diet Coke. Didn't mind it.

Dan went on: "The new chalet is not a convention center—with ten meeting rooms in the main buildings, we're already covered there. But the big thing these days is corporate retreats. Our retreat chalet has a nice open area for presentations and three mini-conference rooms for breaking into smaller groups. And the guests can stay right there—ten suites. We even cater the food over, to keep that retreat feel going."

"Is that where your Cayman Islands seminar will be held?"

That froze him. He'd been all excited, sharing his big plans, and now I'd thrown him a curve. Or maybe hit him with a fastball.

I hadn't seen him look this flummoxed since it turned out an ace of spades was my hole card.

He asked, "How the hell do you know about *that*, Jack?"

"The Bunnies may be gone, but I still date the occasional waitress. Where else is a girl to sleep, when the Bunny Dorm is gone?"

That of course was bullshit. I suppose Dan had mentioned the retreat chalet before, but it hadn't got on my radar, because ...why would it?

Sheer bluff.

"Well," he said, almost whispering now, as if there was anyone around to overhear, "that's not something we're advertising, the seminar. It's really a confidential affair. I hope you haven't mentioned it to anybody."

"Why would I?"

"Just please don't."

I leaned in chummily. "Who are these people, anyway, Dan? Don't tell me this is about giving offshore banking advice to the Outfit crowd."

He looked pale suddenly. My wisecrack hit close to home, which I'd meant it to. "This isn't…this isn't why you wanted to see me this afternoon, Jack…is it? I don't see how this event has anything to do with you."

"Maybe I'd like to participate."

His eyes tightened, as if he were having to work to keep them from falling out of his head. "What do you mean, participate?"

"To attend. To avail myself of the opportunity to learn. To better myself."

He was studying me like I just told him I was thinking of asking his sister out. His thirteen-year-old sister.

"Jack," he said, still very quiet, "don't be ridiculous. You make a nice living, I'm sure, at Wilma's. Not what you could make if you'd take my advice and sell out to those investors I told you about. But we're talking about an 'invitation only' seminar designed for people with *real* money."

Now we were there.

Now it was about to get tricky.

Now there would be no turning back.

Oh, I wasn't going to tell my buddy anything even vaguely approaching the truth. But my lies needed enough weight to get through to him. My lies would be worse than most people's truth.

I asked, "What do you think I do for a living, Dan?"

The pale, handsome features took on quiet alarm. "What do you mean? You run a restaurant-hotel set-up."

My mouth twitched a smile. "I don't *really* run it, though, do I? I mean, I putter, but I leave most of it to my man Charley and a few others. What is it I do for *a living*?"

"…You sell veterinary medicine, don't you?"

"Drugs for cows and horses and puppy dogs?"

"I suppose."

"What if it was drugs for a bigger form of animal?"

His dark eyes were moving side to side, processing.

Then he whispered, "Is that what you do?"

I sipped rum and Diet Coke. "What I do makes it desirable for me to attend that seminar. Isn't that enough? Is there a charge?"

He sucked air in, let it back out. "Everything was prepaid by the attendees." A nervous smile. "Look, Jack, you couldn't attend if you wanted to."

"I *do* want to."

He waved that off. "Well, I mean…you couldn't attend if *I* wanted you to. The enrollment was cut off at five participants."

"I happen to know one of those individuals won't be attending."

He looked at me unblinkingly, his mouth open. If he knew about Vanhorn's murder, he didn't say so. But he didn't not say so.

I said, "I had a business partner named Vanhorn. Silent partner, but now he's *really* silent. He was killed last night. It's been on the news. WGN had the story this morning. I want to take his place at the party. Can you think of a reason why I shouldn't?"

You can almost always tell when somebody's mind has been blown, and this was one of those times.

This very confident man in the Pucci Chicago suit said, "I… I…I…"

"Take your time, Dan."

"I…I guess I can…help you out with this."

"Good. I'll have a woman with me, no one you know. Most presentable. Very professional. Is that a problem?"

"No." He shook his head but it was almost a shiver. "Several attendees will be accompanied by, uh, female guests."

"Not wives, I'm guessing."

"Not wives." He reflected for a moment. "All right. You can attend in Mr. Vanhorn's place."

"Under his name? That doesn't seem like a good idea."

"No! It wouldn't be. But no one is attending under his own name. Everyone's Brown or Jones or Smith or Johnson or...you follow."

"I do. Do you recall Mr. Vanhorn's nom-de-plume?"

"Not off the top of my head, I don't. But I'm checking each of them in, personally, though not in the lobby. Guests have arranged to go directly to the chalet. It has a private parking lot and drive. Nice view of the golf course, with Mountain Top backdrop."

That was the hill people skiing here tried to talk themselves into thinking was a mountain.

"So I'll handle your check-in," Dan said, "and all the details."

"All of a sudden," I said, "I rate."

His expression was numb. "All of a sudden, Jack...you rate."

## ELEVEN

The chalet itself couldn't have been more Alpine if a late-teens Heidi with a bursting peasant blouse had greeted us with a tray of brimming beer steins. The oversize log cabin, the upper two of its three floors sporting building-width railed wooden balconies, sat against pines still touched with snow. Beyond was farmland, barns and silos and such, but all that was largely hidden from view.

Looming over the chalet, a 1,100-foot hill, complete with ski lifts, had its many trails demarcated by landscaping, fir and other trees; the currently snow-patchy, ridiculously named Mountain Top, wore pine borders at far left and far right, like sideburns ascending to an evergreen crown extending all the way across.

Lu and I had taken the time to pick up my Firebird in Muskego and sell back my Impala to my used car guy there. We had decided neither the Camaro nor the Impala would look right in a lot filled with the kind of high-end rides the other attendees would likely roll up in.

I'd also done some clothes shopping. This would not be a t-shirt and jeans affair. Best I could do was the Chess King at Parkland Mall. Probably too hip for the room, and not exactly Brooks Brothers, but I was the right age to get away with the pair of tapered dark suits I picked up—as well as several shiny medium-color shirts and solid-color skinny ties.

Lu needed no help with her wardrobe, starting out in a hot pink jumpsuit with a sash at the waist, hair brushing her shoulders, around which was a neon pink ski coat. For now I was in my black leather jacket from home, and a black-and-white tropical print shirt, also from Chess King.

Our overnight bags strap-slung over our shoulders, we left the Firebird in the small paved (and otherwise empty) lot fronting the chalet. This was almost exactly twenty-four hours after yesterday's meeting with Dan, who greeted us at the lower level's door. As the parking lot indicated, we were the first to arrive. A seven o'clock supper was on the docket, after which the seminar would begin with an introductory session.

"Most of tomorrow," Dan had told me, "will be taken up by a morning session, then individual meetings between our attendees and our guest lecturer."

"The investment 'guru,'" I said.

Dan nodded. "The rest of the weekend will be recreational."

"How so? No skiing, no golf, and you're sequestering the guests here for the duration, right?"

"We have entertainment tomorrow night."

"Oh?"

"Buddy Greco and a trio."

I frowned. "A name artist? How many are attending this thing?"

"Just five, like I said, including yourself. And not including the female guests."

"So ten people get Vegas entertainment? That must have cost a fortune."

"Not a big deal, Jack. Not when the participants are looking to squirrel away cash in the Caymans."

Once Lu and I stepped inside, we were immediately in the main room, which lacked the high ceiling of a lodge, instead with claustrophobic, low-riding open beams; wood was everywhere, a wheat-stained pine—ceilings, walls, floors, even heavily framing the fireplace. Floor-to-ceiling windows provided a view of the golf course whose still-frozen-over water hole made for a sort of lake view. The windows were to your back as you faced the fireplace, which was going, and over which redundantly hung a framed oil of this very chalet, against its Mountain Top backdrop.

Despite the low ceiling, the room was spacious, and the obvious setting for the presentation the Cayman Islands guru would make. Two long low-slung dark blue sofas faced each other over a throw carpet with images of ducks and geese and pheasants flying on a light blue sky, fleeing invisible hunters. A smaller, lighter-blue couch, with its bigger brothers to its left and right, those tall windows to its back, looked across the hunting-scene carpet toward the fireplace.

Dan—in another Gucci of Chicago suit I'd wager, a tan number this time with a yellow, collar-open shirt—carried a clipboard with him and had me initial a few places. Seemed I was registered as William Wilson, and Lu as Mrs. Wilson.

Dan smiled and nodded at Lu, giving me a raised eyebrow glance that said, *Nice going, buddy*, and handed me a room key—305.

"Elevator back with the conference rooms," he said, gesturing vaguely, "but also stairs off the kitchen through there."

"There" was to the left as you faced the fireplace, a farmhouse-style dining area with intentionally clunky carved-wood chairs around two big round matching tables. I asked Dan, "When do you expect the others?"

"Around dark," he said. "No one attending the seminar is anxious to be seen. Yourself included, I'd imagine…Mr. Wilson."

He was right. Checking in here, and not at the desk of the main lodge, meant no one local would notice my presence. After all, I had dated some of the waitresses, and I still took an occasional lunch or dinner here. Dan also let me use the pool, in off-times—even let me keep a locker on site. So assorted staffers knew me as a semi-regular.

And while I was no local celebrity, some folks did know me from Wilma's. Best thing all around for William Wilson was to slip in and out of the chalet, like the rest of the high-class sneaks.

We took the stairs off a modest modern kitchen encased in rustic wood—as Dan indicated, these retreats were primarily catered from the main lodge—and dominated by a long table. Though Lu and I were still lugging our shoulder-slung overnight bags, we took the stairs because I wanted to get the layout of the place down. With all that wood, and the inherent fire hazard, I figured there'd be another stairway somewhere, but no—just the one, and the small elevator.

Our guest room was more of the wood-dominated same—floor, walls, open-beamed ceiling, even rough-hewn furnishings, as well as our own wood-framed fireplace, already burning wood (something unsettling about that). Saving grace was the queen-size bed with faux-fur coverlet, a few light-color throw rugs and some cut flowers in vases almost making up for the deer-hoof lamp with a nature-scene pictorial shade that might have depicted its former owner (of the hooves, not the lamp).

"Is it my imagination," I asked, tossing my black leather jacket on a chair, "or does it smell like a cedar chest in here?"

Lu was already unpacking. She had brought half a dozen handguns, mostly small but very much serviceable, which she was salting around. Here a Colt Auto .25, there a Garcia Berretta Model 70S—little weapons wrapped in underthings in a drawer, or beneath a folded open book on the nightstand. How about a Walther PPK/S .22 under a pillow, or maybe Smith and Wesson .22 in a bathroom soap dish?

Me, I just had my nine mil, which was in a shoulder holster I rarely used and which had required me at the mall to buy a bigger size suitcoat than I preferred.

I sat on the bed. "What exactly do you think we're in for?"

"No idea," she said, still fussing with her guns.

"None?"

"Well…somebody killed Vanhorn and his two boys the other night and the ones on the receiving end didn't seem to be ready for it. We *should* be."

I nodded. "Not sure what the program is myself. I do know that the women attending—other than yourself, my dear—are not married to the participants. This leads me to believe you may be excluded from the seminar."

She was hiding the Berretta. "Most likely. Not that I give a damn. They sound like a bunch of chauvinistic pigs."

"Ah, then you *haven't* stopped subscribing to the feminist newsletter."

That made her smile. She shut the dresser drawer and came over and sat next to me.

Right next to me.

She nibbled my ear and asked, "Are you still the kind of man who reads *Playboy*?"

"Yeah. But also *Hustler* and *Climax*."

"Gynecology fan, huh?"

"Big fan."

"Prove it."

She stripped out of the pink jumpsuit and, naked as a grape, she bent her bare bottom toward me as she neatly folded the garment and laid it over a rough-wood chair with furry upholstery. She had some, too. Then she climbed onto the bed and put her head on a pillow and her hands behind her head, elbows winged, and spread her legs wide.

"Let me know," she said, "if you see anything you like."

After a frozen moment, I dropped trou and—climbing onto the bed awkwardly, using my knees mostly, my pants around my ankles—scrambled over and had a look. Spread the petals and *really* had a look....

Then I buried my face and my tongue went searching and she began to giggle and laugh and squirm. The laughter eased into something else entirely, as did the squirming, and then she was saying, "Why don't you get up here and fuck me, you big hairy ape."

I did.

It didn't take long, but it was energetic and she seemed to like it.

I rolled off and tried to catch my breath.

"We better clean up," she said.

I said something unintelligible, even to me.

She said, "Come on, you lazy lout. Time to eat."

Again, already?

After a quick shower, I got into my new black suit with skinny silver tie and shiny gray shirt, looking sharper than a mannequin at Chess King. Lu, back in her pink jumpsuit and now wearing black spike heels, stood at the window.

"Take a look at this," she said with a nod, arms folded over her shelf of bosom.

I came over and did as she said, gazing out into the dreamlike dusk.

My assumption that the other participants would arrive in various expensive rides, BMWs maybe or Mercedes or even a Porsche or two, had missed the mark. A black Cadillac Fleetwood, a stretch limo with the *de rigueur* tinted windows, was pulling in, making my black Firebird look like a kiddie toy.

A door was held open by a burly chauffeur in black full-length topcoat. But he was pulled up close enough to the building that the passengers he was about to let out were not bothering with coats, though it was cold enough for breaths to smoke.

First to step out was a beautiful woman. Blonde, bosomy, in a leopard print, off-shoulder cheetah dress.

"Patrick Kelly," Lu whispered.

"She doesn't look like a Patrick to me," I said.

"That's who she's wearing," she said patronizingly.

"Oh," I said, and another beautiful woman climbed out.

This was a brunette with big frizzy hair and bright red lipstick, her bosom straining at the metallic liquid gold blouse, her skirt a black midi.

"Michael McNally," I said.

"She doesn't look like a Michael to me," she said.

"Well, she is one. Like that actress. She was also runner-up Playmate of the Year in '75. Or maybe '76."

"Must be old home week for her," Lu said, unimpressed.

The next beauty out, black, wearing a red leather jumpsuit and an Afro that stopped just short of ridiculous, might have been Pam Grier's stand-in. After that came a redhead with a nice slender body, top-heavy with implants, probably, but stunning in any case, in a denim jumpsuit.

"Maybe," I said, "*I* could have worn jeans."

"No. They don't look the same on you."

No argument.

Then came a parade of non-beautiful people.

Men in suits just as sharp as Dan's. Men in their fifties. No topcoats, being dropped off just outside the chalet to head right in, as they were. Wearing sunglasses, though the sun had set—on the day and on them. One with a fat face, another with a narrow one. This one wrinkled, this one a victim of a bad facelift.

And none in ties—all open collar, like Dan. Pastel shirts. Young at heart, these old fucks.

Even two floors up, we could hear them coming in. Out the window, the cauliflower-ear chauffeur was gathering luggage from the trunk, getting ready to haul the stuff in.

"Let's wait till they get settled," I said.

Lu agreed.

A TV hiding in a corner, as if ashamed of itself for existing in such an indoor outdoor paradise, gave us an *Andy Griffith* rerun to watch and then the Chicago news. No mention of the late Envoy.

"That was fast," she said.

I knew what she meant. Said, "Looks like the murders in Wilmette are old news already."

"Else somebody put the lid on."

We'd heard our new neighbors in the hallway moving in. Before too long, out our window, we noticed the beefy chauffeur and the stretch limo taking off, which surprised me a little —you might think this group would feel the need for a security man. Not that it had done Charles Vanhorn any good.

Now, after some relative quiet, came muffled conversation out there indicating everybody was finally heading down to supper. Lu and I waited till the talk subsided, then we went out and took the stairs again.

In the kitchen, everybody was at a buffet line set up at that long table. A chef and a male staffer were serving things up, and neither had faces I knew, so that was one small break, anyway. Dan was back there, too, handing out plates and silverware-in-napkins, answering questions, chatting with the men as they went through the line, not pushing it, just playing genial host. Oddly, the men were lined up first, as a group, and the women after, the females mere side dishes at this banquet, apparently.

That made me the only male here who'd made sure his female companion went before him. Was I committing some reverse etiquette faux pas?

The fare included prime rib, whitefish, and pepper steak over rice, various veggies and potatoes, apple and cherry crisp for dessert. A Styrofoam ice chest was brimming with cans of beer and soda. No other alcohol was on hand for the retreat. They were roughing it, I guess.

In that spirit, the men had their coats off, having left them in their rooms. Trying to fit in, I'd only managed to be out of place—I was that goofball in his shirt and tie who let his woman go in front of him!

I discreetly removed my offending tie, slipped it into a pocket, and opened my collar. Lu and I exchanged a few quick wide-eyed looks through all this. It was like sneaking into a Moose Lodge and not knowing the secret handshake.

In the rustic adjacent dining room, the former Playmate, the blonde, the redhead and Pam Grier's stand-in sat at the near round table, not talking much. The men were at the other table. As we passed that first group, the young women gave me confused looks, as if a nude guy had wandered into their convent. Lu settled into one of the chairs with the beauties; she fit in fine. Those Asian eyes narrowed at me just a little, confirming my own opinion that I needed to join the men without her.

So I went over to an empty chair between the guy with the bad plastic surgery and the fat-faced fuck. Nobody was wearing sunglasses now, and they seemed to know each other, yet they really weren't talking any more freely than they might have had the women joined them.

In a lull in the conversation—which as conversation went wasn't much of anything, apparently the topic being how poorly the chauffeur drove, and why such a convoluted route?—I said, "Evening, gents. I'm William Wilson."

They looked at me. Every single one. They all put down their fork or knife or whatever silverware they happened to be holding and, if they were chewing, swallowed. It was a group glower. They were the jury and I had just copped to an ax murder on the witness stand and punctuated the confession with a big loud fart that echoed in the courtroom.

I said, with a smile that tried hard not to try too hard, "And who are you, gents? Let's go to left to right."

Silence.

The plastic surgery guy, next to me (on my left, so my suggestion wasn't so outrageous after all), said, "Are we going to do this now? I thought we might finish supper first."

He had been a good-looking man once. He was almost a good-looking man twice. But that plastic surgery had pulled the flesh of his face just a little too tight, like a plump woman wearing a dress a size too small with no girdle.

"Before doing what?" I asked. I put just a little edge in it.

They were in their shirtsleeves and I'd taken enough of a look at them to see they weren't packing, or if they were it was something small, like the pop guns Lu hid around our room. I had a nine mil under my arm and could shoot these bastards twice over.

"Those names," the plastic-surgery guy said, "we checked in under? They're only for that purpose."

His hair had started out black, and it still was, but needed help. His eyes were green—like the green felt of my poker table back at the A-frame—and his nose was straight and plastic-surgery perfect and his capped white teeth could smile nice, I bet. Right now they weren't. Smiling nice.

Though they were smiling.

"I'm Henry Poole," he said. "My friends call me 'Hank.' Like Henry Fonda. People say I look like him, some."

"I can see that."

"And this is Alex Kraft," Poole said, gesturing to the fat-faced fuck.

Kraft had skimpy blond hair and little tiny light-blue eyes in pouches and puffy little lips and no chin to speak of. His face was pale with some reddish mottling.

I said, "Mr. Kraft."

Nothing.

"Over there is Joe Field," Poole said, and gestured to the narrow-faced man, who was slender, brown-haired, brown-eyed, with something of a jut to his chin. His tan was dark and, I think, fake.

I nodded to Field.

"And this is George Callen."

Callen was very wrinkled, though not any older than these others, I didn't think. My guess was weight loss. His hair was dark blond and combed-over. He had big dark blue eyes that threatened to burst from the pouches. An ugly man.

I nodded to him, as well.

"But the problem, Mr. William Wilson," Kraft said, "is that you are *not* Charles Vanhorn."

"No one is, anymore," I said.

The four faces looked blankly at me. Poole had his steak knife in his fist, resting on the table.

"You must know that Charles Vanhorn was murdered day before yesterday," I went on cheerfully. I began cutting my prime rib. My knife would stay in hand for a while, too. "Him and the two guys who were protecting him. Poorly."

Poole almost smiled. "That doesn't explain your presence."

"I was Vanhorn's partner," I said. "But this hostile welcome from you gentlemen makes me think I probably shouldn't give you any name other than one you have right now."

"His partner, you say," Poole said.

"That's right. Silent partner. Now he's my really silent partner."

"You killed him?"

"No. Did you?"

Of the four, only Poole did not respond by letting his jaw drop open, at least a little.

"I came here," I said, "because I have the same interest in the possibilities of offshore banking in the Caymans that my late partner had."

"*That's* why you're here," Poole said.

"That's why I'm here," I said with a shrug, and cut my prime rib for another bite.

A doorbell rang and Dan came quickly out of the kitchen, nodding at his guests, and going to answer it.

"I wonder," Kraft said, frowning, "who that could be."

I said, "Not Charles Vanhorn."

Then Dan was back and with him was a handsome black man in the nicest suit in the place, double-breasted gray with an olive silk tie on a striped dress shirt. Tailored, not Chess King.

"Gentlemen," Dan said with a smile and with an open-handed gesture to the newcomer, his other hand on the African-American's shoulder, "this is our seminar leader… Seymour M. Goldman."

Oy vey.

## TWELVE

Dan ushered the handsome, impeccably attired financial guru around the table, where he was introduced to the individual seminar participants, each of whom stood and shook his hand, nodded, smiled. Myself included. To Goldman's credit, though, he had first paused at the ladies' table to smile and half-bow. They looked at him the way a chubby teenage girl looks at a chocolate sundae.

With the exception of Lu, of course, who already had the man of her dreams handy.

As far as those introductions went, the real names of the attendees—not their phony check-in "John Smith" aliases—were not only given to Goldman, but already known to him.

Poole, who seemed to be the table's spokesman, gestured to an empty chair and said, "Help yourself to the buffet, Mr. Goldman, and then join us, if you would."

"Thank you," Goldman said, with another half-bow, displaying a charming Caribbean-tinged English accent, "but I have already eaten and should prepare for tonight's presentation."

I'd had my fill too, of the food and of the tight-lipped company at this table, and rose and said, "Happy to give you a hand, Mr. Goldman."

"Very kind, Mr. Vanhorn." Which was the name I'd given him when I could see everybody was dropping the "John Smith" routine. And though my fellow attendees knew I wasn't Vanhorn, of course, that was the name Goldman and Dan (as far as anybody knew) expected to hear.

The financial guru had a high-end rental ride outside—a

silver Olds Cutlass, fitting for an offshore pirate, I thought—and from there I helped him haul in an easel and some big cards with graphs and charts and a few mounted posters of his beautiful island paradise, to spice up the boredom of how to dodge taxes.

We did this quickly, as it was colder out now and we hadn't bothered with a coat or anything. Back inside, I pitched in, setting up, which included wheeling around, from where it had been tucked against a hallway wall, a cart with a TV and a professional videotape player, provided by the lodge.

"I need to tell you," I said, "that I am *not* Charles Vanhorn."

"Actually," he said, with that crisp appealing accent and a flash of smile, "I knew that. Word of Mr. Vanhorn's demise reached me when I arrived in Chicago this afternoon. But I'm afraid I must insist upon an explanation."

I noticed he hadn't insisted until after I helped him haul his shit in.

"I'm the late Mr. Vanhorn's business partner," I said. "I was aware of this meeting and thought it best I fill in."

"I see." He frowned. "Well…actually I *don't* see. With your business partner dying so recently, I would think you would have other, better things to do."

"Well, I *am* interested in what banking has to offer in the Caymans," I lied. "But I'm also here because of the circumstances of Mr. Vanhorn's demise, as you put it."

His eyes narrowed, his head cocked. "I understand that the circumstances are…troubling."

"Murder usually is. I don't know for sure, but I strongly suspect that one or more of your participants here were responsible for that demise."

"Oh my."

The mildness of his reaction made me smile. "I don't think

you're in any danger, Mr. Goldman, but it's only fair that you know there are underlying circumstances here."

"I understand, Mr., uh…?"

"We can get to my real name later." No we wouldn't. "For now, it's better that you call me Vanhorn."

"*Mister* Vanhorn," he corrected with a smile.

He was a cool customer, all right.

"Might help me to know," I said, "who arranged this seminar —who requested it?"

He took a few moments to consider his reply. "My understanding is that Mr. Poole, representing this small consortium of business associates, through our friends in Chicago, arranged things with their hotel here."

I figured I knew what "Chicago friends" he meant, but I hadn't realized Hefner had been bought out by the Outfit. Not that I was exactly shocked.

Everything was set up and ready for the presentation, so I figured I better get back to the table with my ugly friends. Maybe a second helping of cherry crisp was in order.

But first I asked the guru, "So—is Goldman an alias? If you don't mind my asking."

He laughed. "I don't mind, and it isn't. I actually *am* Seymour M. Goldman, Jr. My mother was native to the Caymans, my father wasn't. I take after my mother. She's a Catholic and so am I."

"Hey, some of my best friends are Catholic."

Another laugh, then a shrug. "But, I have come to find, as the representative of banking interests in the Caymans? My name can be…helpful."

Before the presentation began, Lu and the other females were sent off to their respective rooms. Time for the meeting of the He-Man Woman Haters Klub—no Girlz Allowed. Dan was still around, supervising the clearing of the kitchen, making sure everybody had what they needed.

But he did not attend the first session of the seminar, pausing to make an announcement at the door, on his way back to the main lodge.

"I hope this retreat is a profitable one for all concerned," he said with a smile. "I'm staying on site throughout your weekend, so if you have any needs, just call the desk."

The four booking agents of murder paired off on the facing couches by the fire, in front of which the easel and the TV on its stand were positioned. I had the couch with the windows to my back, facing Goldman and his dog-and-pony show.

Tonight was just an opening salvo and, accordingly, brief. In that charming English-Caribbean accent, the financial guru explained the development of what he termed "bank secrecy" in the Cayman Islands, whose government worked hard at preserving its financial industry's integrity. On the TV a short travelogue played, with the expected sun and sand and ocean representing "the Cayman Islands, a British colony only an hour by jet from Miami."

But the key selling point came quick—that this colony was "free from all forms of direct taxation and currency constraints." The country's laws were designed to invite international business with a minimum of regulatory control.

It was a broad strokes introduction, flavored with facts and figures—500 banks now operated in the Cayman Islands, and 16,000 businesses were incorporated there—and the participants were listening with the rapt attention of guys in the front row of a strip club. But this wasn't about stuffing dollar bills in G-strings. This was about a lot more G's than that, but it was dollars, all right. Lots of them.

After about an hour, Goldman wrapped up, saying tomorrow

morning he would detail various options they might like to consider, followed in the afternoon by one-on-one consultations and recommendations.

Poole stood and led a round of applause, hollow in the low-ceilinged, open-raftered room.

"Great job, Mr. Goldman," he said. All that plastic surgery gave his grin a Phantom of the Opera tinge. "Wonderful stuff. Could you get, uh, Mr. Vanhorn's help again, and clear your things out of the way for now? We have some serious partying to do."

I was Mr. Vanhorn, remember, even though everybody knew I wasn't.

While I helped Goldman move his gear off to a corner, Poole stood in front of the fireplace, saying to his fellow murder brokers, "Go up and get your girls, fellas. I'll do the same. And, trust me, we'll have more than beer tonight to help us celebrate."

Kraft asked, "Celebrate what, Hank?"

Poole shrugged. "Having more than beer."

I went up to the third floor to fetch Lu. She was watching a *Murder, She Wrote* rerun as she sat in one of the rough-hewn, fur-cushioned chairs we'd pulled over earlier.

I sat next to her. "I guess we're partying this evening."

"You learn anything much from that Guess-Who's-Coming-to-Dinner Jew?"

"He's Catholic, actually. Yeah. I learned it's good to be rich. Did you learn anything from the sewing society?"

Her eyes were still on the tube, where the mystery was getting explained by Angela Lansbury. "I did. Seems only the also-ran Playmate of the Year has any kind of ongoing relationship with anybody. She's Poole's mistress. Old-fashioned word, huh? Better than shack job, I guess. The others are working girls."

I frowned. "I never saw street corners with the likes of them."

"And you won't. We're talking high-ticket call girls. I gather they are from the Outfit's typing pool. Only they don't type."

"None with history with any of my fellow chauvinists downstairs?"

"I didn't say that. I think these girls have been escorts for most of those beasts before. Just aren't going steady with any of 'em, shall we say."

"They aren't going down to the malt shop together."

"Just going down."

"Let's us go down. Downstairs, that is."

We did, taking the stairs again, with music coming up to greet us—"Like a Virgin," which is what the four beauties were dancing to. Unintentional irony or smug sarcasm? You decide.

In any case, the flying pheasant carpet between the two couches had flown, the seating scooched back to make more room for the girls to dance. The beauties had not changed the outfits they'd worn on arrival, with the partial exception of the redhead, who had removed her denim jacket to reveal a neon lime-and-gray t-shirt with a plunging neckline, to show off the boobs she had undoubtedly bought. And worth every penny, I'd say.

"Join in," I whispered in Lu's ear.

She nodded and got to dancing with the other babes. Or boogieing or whatever the fuck they were calling it. These kids today.

The couch by the windows where I'd sat earlier had been shoved to one side, and in its place sat a big blocky wooden table with bottles of gin, vodka, rum and bourbon. A tower of red Solo cups and an ice bucket shared the space, and on the floor next to the table squatted the Styrofoam chest of iced soda and beer. Also on the floor back there was the source of the music, a big boom box, really cranked.

Poole, who already seemed a little drunk, brayed over the sounds, "Help yourself, kiddies! I got plenty more upstairs if we run dry!"

Obviously Poole had come prepared to violate the notion that only soda and beer would be served at the retreat. Not being a rule breaker by nature, I helped myself to a can of Diet Coke.

On the left, as I faced the dancing girls, pudgy Kraft sat next to skinny Field—the worst Laurel and Hardy impersonators ever. On the right sat pruneface Callen, alone at the moment. I joined him.

"The Power of Love" started up, a song I actually liked. Huey Lewis. Now and then one of the girls would pogo to it. Worse things to watch in the world.

I said to Callen, "We need to talk."

The wrinkled face managed to convey what we all know: those four words, strung together like that, are nothing anybody wants to hear. Especially from a lover, but also from somebody attending a murder bookers convention, however exclusive.

"About?" he asked. Even his voice sounded wrinkled.

"I wanted to give you some food for thought."

"Not especially hungry."

"How about a warning? Can you make room in your belly for that?"

His eyes were cold and dark and hard, nothing at all like their saggy settings. His nod was barely there. But it was there, all right.

I said, "I think my business partner, Vanhorn, was murdered by one of us."

"What the hell are you talking about?"

"The five of us who broker murder contracts. Does that spell it out enough?"

The barely there nod again.

I went on: "I think somebody among us is trying a power play. I think one of us killed Vanhorn as an opening gambit. For a wholesale takeover of our business. To become one overall broker."

"Impossible," he said, and huffed a sneering laugh. "Ridiculous. There are a good two dozen of us operating in the continental United States alone. We *need* regional set-ups."

"Where do you work out of, George?"

"Milwaukee."

"Vanhorn was in Wilmette. Which is Chicago. Do you know where Hank and Joe and Alex operate from?"

A shrug. "Cleveland. St. Louis. Des Moines."

"Midwest. A good chunk of it, anyway."

Again the barely there nod.

I said, "Somebody's trying to take over the region."

His eyebrows tensed, making his forehead wrinkle even more. "You have proof?"

"Just a friendly heads-up. Remember me, if my warning works out well for you."

He shrugged again, but those cold dark eyes were moving in thought. Barely moving. But moving.

I had similar conversations with the others. Whether any of them figured out what I was doing—noticing that I'd quietly buttonholed each of them in the noise—I couldn't tell you. But the subject even seemed to sober Poole up. Temporarily.

"A power play?" he said, gesturing with his sloshing Solo cup. We were standing off to one side, talking over "Everybody Wants to Rule the World" (I swear) but with no one close enough to hear us over it. "You can't be serious."

"What part of Vanhorn shot in the head can't you buy?"

The eyes narrowed in that face of stretched skin. He leaned close. "This is a dangerous line of enterprise we're in." He was slurring now. "Vanhorn could've alienated our Chicago 'sociates. How should *I* know?"

"Maybe you better find out."

He shrugged and spilled a little booze. "Coulda been a straight-up home invasion, y'know. Place is isolated enough, wealthy area. If there's anything to it, Chicago will let us know."

"Unless Chicago's behind it. Maybe they want their own people in and independents like us out."

The capped teeth flashed. "Indies like *you*? I didn't even know who the fuck you *are*, Mr. Will-i-am Wilson. I never heard anything about Vanhorn having a silent partner."

"That's why you don't hear anything. They're silent."

"Why don't you *stay* that way?"

And he scowled and drifted off.

By the time "Sussudio" by Phil Collins came on, I'd talked to them all, and Poole was not the only one drunk enough to imagine he could dance—they all did. It was funny for a while. Then at a certain point you were embarrassed to be human. This did not seem to be a species worth belonging to.

A slow song started up—"You Give Good Love," Whitney Houston—and the four men danced with, or was that dry-humped, their dates. Ah romance.

The former runner-up Playmate of the Year was getting publicly pawed in an embarrassing, overt way by the now very drunk Poole. One hand on her ass, the other on a breast. When the song finally stopped, she squirmed out of his grasp and pushed him away and ran off. Crying maybe.

Poole grinned at everybody, since we'd all become his audience, and shrugged and said, "Chicks!" In that charming way gentlemen do.

Then, with all eyes on him, Poole reached in a trouser pocket and withdrew a small black-capped bottle of white stuff.

"Anybody interested in dessert?" he asked, and headed toward the dining room.

Everybody followed him, except Lu and me and the most embarrassed guest at the party, Seymour M. Goldman, Jr., who throughout had been awkwardly standing on the periphery with a drink in hand and a frozen smile on his face, and after all, where else would it be?

I went over to him.

"What wise man was it that said," I asked, "are we having fun yet?"

"Zippy the Pinhead," Goldman said, an answer that—especially in his British/island accent—made my estimation of him rise, as did what he said next: "I don't care to be a part of this. Actually, I *can't* be a part of this."

He had a car. Nothing to stop him.

"I was supposed to stay here at the chalet," he said, "but now. . . ."

"Understood," I said. "Will you be back tomorrow?"

"I don't honestly know."

Everybody was in there doing lines on the two round tables, Poole generously pouring out nose candy and everybody was giggling and laughing. Who knew better than I what things go better with?

I said, "Dan Clark would arrange a room for you at the main lodge, I'm sure."

He put a hand on my shoulder and patted it. "I'll find somewhere, Mr. Vanhorn. Thank you. These are *not* conscientious people."

No, really?

But before the guru could leave, Michael McNally—Poole's Playmate playmate—came back from wherever she'd been and grabbed Goldman by both hands. Astonished—whether by her beauty, which was considerable, or the abruptness of it all—he allowed himself to be pulled out to the dance floor, where "Suddenly" by Billy Ocean was playing.

She folded herself into his arms. He was trying to just dance with her, to keep it friendly, but she was drunk and she'd been mishandled by her man, literally manhandled, and before Goldman could extricate himself, Poole came bolting in from coke town and yanked her free and slapped her twice, hard, enough for the blows to be heard above "Wake Me Up Before You Go-Go." Wham.

She screamed and started slapping him back in a flurry, like a child trying to bat away a bully, which is really what she was doing. He grabbed her and started shaking her. Till her teeth rattled, and that's not a figure of speech. It's what you could hear.

Now this is what Goldman did.

He disappeared.

He got out of there so fast and so slippery, I didn't know whether to admire him or run after him to kick his ass.

Now here's what I did.

Nothing.

I wasn't here to be a hero. I was here to watch and listen and do my best not to get killed, with Lu along for the ride. She got it. She was next to me, right next to me, her arm looped in mine. We were just pausing at a cage as we strolled through the zoo. Ah! The monkeys are throwing shit again—best keep our distance.

No, it wasn't a man who finally rode to the rescue. Not one of the other participants at the retreat, either, including yours truly, as I've said. The saviors of the Playmate—her mouth bloody, her big hair even more askew than her stylist had made it—were the high-class whores who came running in, several with powder on their noses, but every one indignant, yelling at Poole and then gathering around the Playmate protectively.

Pam Grier's stand-in yelled at Poole, "We are fucking *out* of here!"

Poole yelled at her, "Well, get the fuck out then!"

My turn.

I stepped up and said, "I'll call Dan. He'll arrange something for them."

Poole, calming a little, said, "Our limo's still here."

"No it isn't."

He made a waving gesture, as if I were a fly. "Not parked here, but our driver is staying over in the main lodge. You make the call, whoever-the-fuck-you-are."

"Since you asked nicely," I said, and went off and used the kitchen phone to call the desk and get Dan.

Within fifteen minutes the young women had gathered their things and were the fuck out of there, to get swallowed up by the same black limo that had earlier disgorged them.

The only female left was mine. Lu. And she was hanging close to me.

Funny thing. Through all of that, nobody had bothered to turn off the music.

Whitney Houston was singing, "The Greatest Love of All."

# THIRTEEN

The subdued lighting in the main lodge's indoor pool reflected the hotel policy of adults only between nine and eleven PM. After hours, at a little before midnight, that twilight ambiance remained, but I didn't have any other adults to put up with, thanks to my "in" with the manager.

I'd called Dan before coming over. "How's our financial guru doing?"

"Not saying much. I gave him a suite and he was polite, but he doesn't seem happy."

"Will he bail?"

"Maybe. Maybe not. The, uh, ladies were picked up safely by the limo, I trust?"

"Yup."

"Any additional drama?"

"Nope."

His chuckle sounded warm, even over the phone. "I have to admit it's kind of nice having you there on the scene, Jack. Your eyes and ears come in handy."

"Glad to be of service. You okay with Lu and me coming over for a midnight swim? Think I need a little time away from this relaxing retreat."

He grunted a laugh. "Don't blame you. Of course you can come over."

"Could you line up a suit for Lu?"

"Glad to. It'll be at the front desk. You still have that key to the pool area?"

I said I did.

Dan had a two-piece suit waiting for Lu at the front desk (I had trunks in my locker), and we had the place to ourselves. The kidney-shaped pool wasn't large, rather overwhelmed in fact by the surrounding cement and endless deck chairs. Not ideal for swimming laps, though that was what I was doing. Nice and easy ones in the warm water.

Funny how, while I did enjoy summer swims in a lake that was after all at my doorstep, I somehow preferred an indoor pool like this, year round. The echo of a big room lending an otherworldly resonançe and the shimmer of water reflecting around the chamber, even the chlorine bouquet burning eyes and twitching nostrils, seemed oddly soothing to me. Probably because it took me back to high school days when I was on the swim team and winning ribbons and trophies that weren't for shooting.

Things at the chalet, it seemed to me, had really gotten out of hand, and the only way I could think it through was to swim. Lu, in a navy two-piece suit that fit her surprisingly well for a loaner, was not doing laps. She was in the hot tub, immersed to her shoulders, arms spread out along the sides, eyes hooded.

After half an hour of laps, I swam slowly over near her, then, treading water, said, "Come join me."

Her smile was sleepy. "You come join me."

"No, that heat will lull me too much. Drowning asleep in a hot tub would only embarrass me."

She smirked. "Risk it."

So I climbed out, toweled off, and slipped down and in and under the water next to her, sitting on a little submerged ledge with a jet working on my lower back.

She purred, "This is a nice break."

"From lunacy. Yes. It is."

A row of high windows was letting in moonlight. Red and

white awnings at this end of the pool, a family friendly touch in post-Playboy Club days, were subdued into submission.

"I thought," she said, "you wanted to stay away from here."

She meant the main lodge.

I said, "I did."

"Because there are people here who know you."

"Yes. But I needed this. And nobody's around, really."

"Okay." She was studying me. "Do you feel like you know any more about what's going on, now that we've crashed the party and stayed a while?"

I frowned. "Maybe 'know' is too strong. But I have the feeling that, with one exception, my seminar buddies don't know about me."

She frowned back. "You mean, that you're the fly in the ointment? The one behind ten years of contracts getting upended, here and there?"

"That, but also they seem to accept my story about being Vanhorn's business partner. These brokers don't work together. Oh, they know about each other. But they're independent businessmen with ties to the Outfit, who feed them jobs. Yet they aren't themselves Outfit."

"That makes a difference?"

"I think so. Your Envoy took over most of the Broker's players. So he felt the squeeze of my interloping, over the years. He had reason to try to understand what was going on, and eventually figure out what I was up to. These other middlemen in murder? No."

"You said an exception. Who?"

"Poole. Something's not right about him."

Her eyebrows hiked. "I'll say. Slapping his honey around like that. Getting soused. Handing out coke like Halloween candy."

I shrugged. "I don't exactly run with this crowd. Maybe that was normal behavior, tonight. Par for the course. Maybe these bland sons of bitches are wild-ass party animals, when they attend something like this—work by day, play at night."

It was her turn to shrug. "Fairly typical convention-goer-type behavior, I'd say."

I nodded again. "But that's not the only thing bothering me about Poole. He had an attitude toward me the others didn't. Skepticism, maybe. Suspicion for sure."

"So what do we do tomorrow? Just let this play out?"

I huffed a sigh. "That's part of what I've been mulling. For one thing, I'm not sure this seminar isn't *already* over. Seymour M. Goldman seemed fairly freaked out. He may head back to tax-dodger paradise."

"Which leaves us where?"

"Not sure," I admitted. "As for right now, we can go back and spend the night, then leave first thing in the morning. Announce that tonight's fun and games were just a little much for us, and go."

"Go where?"

"That is a goddamn good question. Back to my place, to wait to see if anybody comes around to kill me? Back to yours in St. Paul, to wait to see if anybody comes around to kill you? Or do we, together or separately, walk away from those left-handed lives of ours and start over, right-handed? We both have the money for it. Tahiti maybe. You go topless and I'll learn to paint like Gauguin. Maybe sell black velvet paintings of you to tourists."

By the end of that, she was laughing. Not hard, but laughing, though we both knew it was no laughing matter, really.

"Maybe," she said, finally, "*I* should swim for half an hour and think about it."

"There's an aspect of this," I said, "we haven't looked at. What about the list?"

"The list? The Broker's list?"

I nodded. "What if this is an unfriendly takeover, in the business sense? Those four are all working the Midwest. So was Vanhorn. Maybe one of them wants to expand. Take over Vanhorn's market share. In which case he—whoever 'he' is—needs access to the Envoy's roster of friendly neighborhood hired guns."

"Wouldn't he—whoever he was—force that list out of Vanhorn first? Get it out of that wall safe of his? Or get access to it in some way or fashion?"

"Maybe. Maybe not." I lifted my shoulders and put them back down. "If not, then my list becomes really valuable, even with ten years of tire tread worn off it. Or maybe…shit, that could be it!"

"What could?"

I leaned toward her. "If one of my seminar buddies *does* know about me—knows what I've been up to—he'd obviously want to stop me. Stop me from screwing up contracts and bumping off his assets. But maybe he also wants to lay hands on that list, to see if it still has useful assets."

The Asian eyes opened wider than I thought they could. "God. It's starting to look like your only good option is to go home and wait for somebody to come around to kill you. And kill them instead."

"…I'm going to swim some more."

"I'll join you."

She started to climb out, her top-heavy, long-legged frame nicely water-pearled. Funny how ten years later she was even lovelier than she'd been—back then, she'd only been stunning.

I followed her over to the pool and we swam lazy, loping laps for around fifteen minutes. Then, wordlessly, we got out, gathered our handguns wrapped in towels, and went to our appropriate locker rooms.

We had driven over in the Firebird. We walked to the car in

the side parking lot under half a moon and a scattering of clouds and a handful of stars flung carelessly around by a God who didn't care about our problems or what we did about them. The cold felt bracing, after the hot tub and warm pool. With no wind, it really wasn't so bad.

Behind the wheel, with Lu next to me, I glanced over and said, "We could just go. Just ride."

"Into the sunset?"

"Into the dawn, anyway. For now, we don't have to make our minds up. If we don't want to play this game of kill or be killed, fuck it. We have enough money to set up shop somewhere. Antiques is fine. We are not old, lover."

She smiled. "Lover. You never called me that before."

"Well, it's overdue."

I leaned over and kissed her. She kissed me back, as warm as the night was cold. It lasted a while. Then we went to our respective corners, with more rounds left to fight.

"We'll sleep on it," she said.

"Sleep on it," I said with a nod.

I drove over to the chalet, where not a single car was in the lot until I parked mine, close to the entry. No lights on in the place, either, not on any of the three floors.

"Odd," I said.

"Why so?"

"Well, after the coke and music and slapping and screaming... our busy little party animals all seem to be tucked in their wee little beds."

"It's after one, Jack."

I was looking at the chalet like it was a spooky house and our car had broken down, and was it wise to ask for help there? Let's do the Time Warp again.

"I know it's after one," I said. "But nobody's reading in bed, or humping with the lights on or anything? Even a TV would provide some glow. Nobody's rustling around in the kitchen for food? Or a stray line of coke?"

She touched my arm, squeezed. "It's fine. You're getting paranoid. Let's just go in and go to bed. But *that* decides it."

"What?"

Her expression was firm. "We're out of here in the morning. First thing."

"No."

"No?"

The heel of my hand hit the steering wheel. "Tonight. We'll go in, pack up, and follow the example of those working girls. Get the hell out of Dodge."

She thought about it, then nodded.

We went in that first-floor door—all the guests had been given keys to the chalet—and I switched on a light over the entry area. Still mostly in the dark was the big low-ceilinged living room, awash in wood, where all the fun had been had.

For a change, we used the elevator. On the third floor, we went to our room and turned several lights on, which had a settling effect on us, even if the doe-hoof lamp didn't. Nonetheless, my mind hadn't been changed. I began packing and so did Lu, which for her largely consisted of collecting the guns she had salted around.

And *I* was paranoid?

She stepped into one of her jumpsuits and I got back in the black Aloha shirt with white blossoms and my lined black leather jacket and black jeans, the nine millimeter in the deep jacket pocket. I noticed she was carrying her little Smith and Wesson .22 in a palm.

Soon, like guests trying to duck the bill, we crept out of our room and I almost missed it.

Almost missed it because I had been wrong—somebody *did* have a light on. I hadn't noticed when we'd got off the elevator and quickly made it to our room, probably because the half-open door was off to the side, and the light within probably wasn't more than a nightstand lamp.

We were waiting for the elevator when something made me go over and check it out.

"Jack," she whispered, "what are you doing?"

"Not sure," I said, something prickling at the back of my neck. I was getting my nine mil out.

With the toe of my right Reebok, I nudged the door open just a little. Just a tad. Not much at all.

But enough to see him sprawled on the floor.

"Jack," she whispered, not having the view I did. "Elevator's here."

I summoned her with a curled finger.

She came over, frowning, then as I shouldered the door gently open, her eyebrows went up and her jaw went down. I slipped inside and she followed, shutting the door quietly behind her with an elbow. For a good ten seconds, which is longer than it sounds, we just stared.

Pudgy Alex Kraft, in yellow pajamas and brown slippers, was on his back and he was staring at the open-beamed ceiling with three eyes. Well, really two eyes and a red hole in his forehead. His hands were over his head, as if he were doing a prone jumping jack, though I doubted he'd ever done one standing up. His weak-chinned, blond fuzz-topped head lay in a little lake of blood, still glistening red.

This had happened not long ago. Probably not while we were in the building, although that was not impossible. But not long ago.

I checked the bathroom and the closet, and even under the bed, then glanced at Lu and shook my head.

Nobody.

We used our sleeves to wipe off anything we'd touched, then reconvened in the area by the elevator, which had gotten impatient waiting for us and gone away.

"What now?" she asked, softly but not quite a whisper.

"We could just fucking go," I said, also sotto voce, "and maybe get shot in the back stepping off the elevator or coming down the stairs."

"Or?"

My look told her this was my preferred option. "Check out the rest of this building."

We did that.

In the room next to ours, the door was also cracked open but no lights were on. Enough moonlight was coming in the windows, though, to illuminate George Callen in his bed, sleeping on his side, or anyway he had been when somebody put a bullet in his left temple, turning his pillow an irregular scarlet. He appeared to be in his underwear, but I wasn't about to pull the covers back to confirm that.

She was frowning. "Could all this have *just* happened? Wouldn't we have heard it?"

My nod was slow. "Probably. Even with a silenced gun, the noise in a place this quiet would've got our attention."

"Then you think if this had happened before we left, we'd have heard the shots."

"I think if this had happened before we left," I said, "*we'd* have been shot."

She shuddered, frowned, shook her head as if to clear cobwebs. "So the shooter is gone."

"Let's not get ahead of ourselves."

That left one more room on our floor, which proved to be unlocked, but showing no sign that anyone had slept there. Probably the room Goldman would have used, if he hadn't bailed.

On the second floor, we encountered a locked door. We knocked, got no answer. Probably a room without a guest, including both categories—living and dead.

The next door was locked too, a replay of the previous one.

But another unlocked room came next, only the bed was rumpled, obviously slept in. No sign of a current occupant. So, presumably, one of the seminar participants wasn't in his room.

The last door we tried was ajar on a room offering up another sleeping beauty, only not a beauty and nobody who could be woken with a kiss. Thin-faced Joe Field, in shiny brown pajamas too big for him, appeared to have been shot in the head in his sleep, like Callen. Also a side sleeper, but the other side. Also resting on a blood-soaked pillow.

For the moment, we returned to our room. Sat on the bed with our guns in our laps.

She asked, "Somebody have keys to the rooms? A passkey maybe?"

"Maybe. Or just as likely got let in, because the person knocking was another seminar participant, stopping by for some conversation or whatever. Who then left the door unlocked without the occupant noticing, or taped it to prevent locking."

She seemed confused, not afraid. "So what do we do? Call the cops?"

"You're funny. No. You notice who isn't among those present? And dead?"

"Poole. The room with the rumpled bed is obviously his. You must be right about him."

I nodded. "And he's probably disappointed he didn't add us to his tally. He could be downstairs waiting."

She shook her head. "No, he would have taken us out when we got here."

"Probably. Shall we risk that?"

"...Maybe not."

I put my hand on her shoulder. "We'll go down and check the lower floor. Make sure that we're alone. You haul your travel bag along. Because then, you're leaving."

"I am?"

"You are. You can meet me at my A-frame or head back to St. Paul, as you please." I got my car keys from my jacket pocket and handed them to her. "Just don't take my Firebird with you if you head back to the Twin Cities, okay? Get some use out of that Camaro."

She nodded, smiled.

We checked the main floor out.

Nothing, nobody.

It was possible we'd just played out a bedroom farce with the shooter, with us coming up and going into our room, and him then coming out of a victim's room and going down. *Fawlty Towers* with guns.

Finally we hustled from the chalet into the parking lot to the nearby Firebird, staying very fucking low.

Then she was gone, with a throaty roar of my car's engine, and I went back in.

Just me and the dead.

# FOURTEEN

I called the front desk at the main lodge and got put through to Dan Clark, who was staying in a room there to be handy in case anything came up at the chalet. I felt like this qualified.

I met him at the door. He'd come over in his dark blue Jaguar sedan, which he didn't look as spiffy as. His short dark hair managed to stick up a little on one side, where he'd slept on it, his face appeared a little puffy, eyes lacked their usual sharpness, and he looked like a guy who'd been woken up in the middle of the night. Which he was, although at after two AM, this really was morning, wasn't it?

He looked more irritated than alarmed by this summons, as he came quickly but unenthusiastically from the parked vehicle to the doorway where I stood, his breath smoking with cold. He hadn't taken time for a topcoat. He was back in the tan tailored suit and yellow, open-collar shirt, but they'd been thrown on.

All I'd told him on the phone was: "Get the hell over here. Quick. Bring nobody."

"What is it?" he'd asked.

"It's bad. Get over here."

Now here he was, and I ushered him in. I'd turned a few lights on but the chalet remained underlit, although while I'd waited for him I'd lighted a fire in the big fireplace downstairs.

"Okay, Jack," he said, "so what the fuck?"

"I'm going to give you a little tour of your facility," I said. "There's been some dramatic remodeling."

He frowned, taking in the emptiness, which didn't back up my implied crisis. "Where is everybody? Asleep?"

"You could say that."

"Do we need to be quiet?"

"Not really."

I showed him around the impacted rooms in the order that Lu and I had made our discoveries, starting on the third floor. Seeing pudgy Kraft in his pj's on his back with a hole in his forehead, and that big blossom of blood framing his noggin, got an immediate reaction out of Dan. Well, a two-part immediate reaction. First the lodge manager froze, deer-in-the-headlights style. Then he ran into the bathroom and knelt at the porcelain altar and made an offering.

I was in the doorway of the john as he stood at the sink, running cold water and splashing it on his face. He toweled off and looked at me, horrified, the angular features of his narrow face twisted into a grotesque grimace, his handsomeness M.I.A.

"Do the others know?" he asked.

"Probably not. You okay?"

"No I'm not okay!"

"There's more to do."

He gripped my arm. "We're not calling the cops. You haven't called the *cops*, have you, Jack?"

"I have not called the cops. What are friends for, Dan? Come on. We're just getting started."

"What?"

I didn't bother answering, just led him past the corpse and out into the hall.

My poker pal took in Callen's bed-bound corpse, and Field's, more stoically. He clearly had nothing left to puke up, and his comments ran to what you might imagine: "Jesus…oh my God… Christ!" Which sounds more religious than it was.

Then we were downstairs, him on one blue couch, me facing him on the other, with the fire crackling and snapping between us at my right and his left, its warmth providing a bizarre coziness, aided and abetted by the moonlight pouring in the tall windows.

I was sitting back, an ankle on a knee, arms along the top edge of the cushions behind me, the lined black leather jacket unzipped. Numb, Dan was sitting forward, knees apart, folded hands draped between his legs, shaking his half-hanging head.

Then something occurred to him, his chin snapping up, the eyes sharp again. "What about Poole?"

The shock of having three corpses as chalet guests finally dulled enough for him to realize the body count was off by one.

"Not here," I said. "Room's empty. I believe he did this."

"What about your girl?"

"Mrs. William Wilson? I sent her off where she might not find things so unpleasant. Hey, things could be worse."

"How in hell?"

I shrugged. "Those guys up there could have shit themselves."

He covered his face with both hands. Not crying or anything. Just wishing this would all go away, I guess.

Then, getting himself together, he dropped his hands to his thighs and sat up straight. He was a professional, after all. An executive.

"Listen, Jack. With your…shall we say, 'veterinarian drugs' business…you certainly don't need the kind of official scrutiny this thing could bring."

"No argument there."

"And if this became known to the public…my God, we'd be finished here. This lodge would be over, unless somebody figured out how to market a Manson Family vacation. And who would ever want to hire me?"

"It's a pisser."

He made a face. "These people…I don't have to tell *you*. You were Vanhorn's 'silent partner,' you said?"

I nodded.

Eyebrows high, he held two palms out, surrender-style. "I don't want to *know* partner in what!"

"Well, crime of course."

"Don't tell me any more, Jack! Don't tell me any fucking more. I know that these people—yourself included—are…connected. In a way, so am I. Chicago money is behind the lodge, you know that, right? And you know what kind of Chicago money I mean."

"I do."

He cocked his head, his voice quiet, reasonable. "So what I propose to do is call a number. I will report what the situation is here, and a clean-up crew will be dispatched. Before anyone gets a whiff of this, before the sun comes the hell up, this will be taken care of. Those things upstairs…" He pointed upward. "…will be gone. Disposed of. Do you understand?"

"I not only understand," I said with a pleasant little smile, "I approve."

He stood. Clapped once. "I'm going to make the call now." He nodded toward the moon-swept parking lot out the windows. "Then I'm going to personally drive you home. We can talk later, but the short version is—none of this ever happened."

"Fine by me."

He sighed, smoothed his suitcoat, which could use it, and went off to the kitchen to use the phone. He spoke softly and I didn't catch exactly every word of what he was saying, but the call was as he described it. Took him no longer than ordering a pizza.

He came back and sat down on his couch across from me, the fire reflecting orange and blue on him. Said, "Won't be more than an hour before they're here."

"Works for me."

He sucked in a bunch of air, then sighed it out. Half-smiled, in that shared private joke way. Then his expression darkened and his forehead tensed.

"Jack, what do you think this was about? Why would Poole have done all this?"

"Your seminar guests were all in the same business, with the same Outfit ties." I was careful not to say what that business was. "But in a way they were competitors, too. I think it was a power play."

He nodded, smiled tightly. "Starting with taking out the Envoy."

Well, that told me that something I'd suspected had been right on the nose, so I got the nine millimeter out of the deep jacket pocket and pointed the gun at him. No silencer, but the chalet was well enough away from the rest of the facility that one little gunshot wouldn't matter much. And that Jag was waiting for me outside for an easy getaway.

All I had to do was squeeze the trigger.

And in retrospect, I should have. It wasn't hesitation over Dan being a poker buddy, though that made this a little sad. No, it was my own goddamn, innate curiosity. I wanted confirmation.

I said, "Had you said 'Vanhorn' and not 'Envoy,' I wouldn't have been sure. I was *fairly* sure, just finding out that this resort is an Outfit property and you're their fair-haired boy. And I think I know why you'd hire to have me killed. But do me a favor and tell me I'm right. And how you knew."

He was shaking his head, frowning even as his eyes grew big. "Knew what? What the fuck are you talking about, Jack?"

"You want Wilma's Welcome Inn. Or the property it lies on, and the rare zoning it enjoys. Shit! You even want my little A-frame and the lot adjoining Wilma's! That would make a real moneymaker, a brand spanking new lakeside facility. Family friendly! In various senses of the word."

"You can't really believe that. Get serious, Jack! We're friends!"

"Right. Because you wormed your way into my poker group six months ago."

He said nothing.

*And I knew what he'd been thinking, or at least thought I did. He came around my corner of the world often enough, dropped by the Welcome Inn for a meal and/or a drink. He was no stranger. Must have asked Charley what kind of family I had, and my loyal employee must have known about my old man being my heir. I'd been kidding myself that the old reprobate wouldn't get curious and look inside that envelope I'd left in his safekeeping. Not* that *safe, apparently.*

"Okay," I said. "So you know about my old man in Ohio, who would have no reason not to sell the property and make his own killing. Do you know why I've had no interest in selling, though?"

Now his curiosity kicked in.

"No, Jack," he said, dropping all pretense. "No idea. It was stupid of you not to."

"So then you don't know," I said, "who, or what, I am."

He shrugged. "I do now. You're just another filthy drug dealer."

I laughed. "No! I'm another filthy contract killer. That lakeside A-frame is my retreat. I'd never sell it."

The blood drained from his face.

"The so-called Envoy knew who and what I was," I said. "I thought maybe he'd told you. Tell me, Dan. Did your Chicago friends just advise you to do your best to pry my property out of me? Or were they behind the contract itself?"

Again, he said nothing.

"I'm guessing the contract was your idea," I said. "I'm guessing you wanted to pick my property up for a relative song, and then go partners with the Outfit."

Had anyone ever moved so fast?

He came at me, and I fired, but the slender son of a bitch only got grazed along his side, gouging his Pucci suitcoat and maybe not his flesh at all, and he'd flung himself at me so hard, he lifted the couch half-off the ground. Both his hands were on the wrist of my gun-in-hand and he twisted the nine mil from my grasp, sending it clattering to the wood floor beyond the hunting rug. I was blocked by the couch arm but he wasn't, and he dove to the floor and had the gun in *his* hand now. He swung the big automatic toward me and I leapt over the facing couch as two bullets thunked into the cushions.

I was scrambling now, and the door to the outside was right there, and I reached up for the knob, twisted it, opened the door and clambered out of there. The cold was startling, like a splash of ice water, and the world was an ivory thing in the moonlight, dark but not dark. In front of me was the parking lot, and beyond that the frozen sort of a lake that was the golf course waterhole.

With no immediate route of escape, which took me a millisecond to compute, I tucked to one side of the door, which I'd left ajar, and waited. He came through moving fast, and you know what? I tripped the motherfucker. He skidded face down on the pavement of the parking lot and I jumped on his back, jamming a knee into the base of his spine. He yelped in pain and now it was my turn to try to wrest my nine millimeter free from *his* grasp, my hands tight and twisting on his wrist. His fingers managed to fling the weapon rather than give it up and it went skittering across the slightly icy pavement and disappeared under his parked Jag.

I scuttled off him to retrieve the gun and knelt to see where the thing had gone—it had spun to a stop under the car. I tried to reach it and something tragic happened: a bullet whanged into the side of the Jag, puckering a beautiful door.

He was still down on the pavement, looking dazed the way you do when a kick in the head hasn't quite knocked you unconscious, but pushing up on his left hand and pointing a little gun at me, a .25 auto I think. Hadn't thought he might be packing, even if it was a dainty little fucking thing like that.

I couldn't reach the nine mil and he would only get less dazed and take better shots, so I had to get away from him fast, and the parking lot and frozen waterhole were shit options.

But off to my left was the start of the thickness of pines that climbed the so-called mountain, and I headed into that cover, fast, thinking only of putting something between me and my pursuer that wasn't cold air.

A ski path angled through the forest of firs, some other non-conifer trees mixed in, skeletal spectators, but it was easy enough to avoid that openness, and the trees weren't planted so close together that I couldn't wind through them. Not to where I could run, but I could manage a jog, all right, and periodically pause behind a tree, many of which were substantial enough for cover.

No additional gunshots had rung out since I had fled frantically into the trees, but I could hear him back there, feet crunching through the snow, not running or jogging but moving quickly enough to stay a threat.

The cold was not a problem—it kept me alert—but running in it was taxing. My breath soon came hard, and plumed in front of me, as if I were one big punctured tire oozing air.

*"Jack!"*

Not close, but closer than I would have liked.

*"Jack, stop! Talk to me! We can work this out!"*

He never could bluff worth a damn.

But without a weapon, I had no goal in sight. Being in first place in a race with a guy in second place who had a gun was no way to win. Maybe I could double back around behind him. The semi-snow-covered ground was a problem, though—especially the leaves and pine cones beneath the snow, which gave away movement. After all, that was how I could have a sense of where, and how far back, Dan was.

So I started working my way over toward the winding ski path. If I stayed along the edge, I wouldn't be so exposed, and anyway Dan wouldn't be expecting me to head back down, not yet anyway. And the going should be less noisy, with fewer pine cones and leaves.

That proved to be the case, while at the same time Dan's crunching grew louder, as he came closer to my new position, but unaware of doing so. I paused when his footfalls got loud enough to indicate he was passing me.

That was when I spotted the broken wooden ski pole, snapped in two. I paused, picked up the half with the metal tip, tossed the other half away, and headed back up, again hugging the side of the ski trail.

The crunching of Dan's feet up ahead grew louder.

Gaining, I cut through the trees and moved toward the sound. When I saw him in the moonlight, his back to me, I slipped in behind him—he was maybe ten yards up there—and walked in his footsteps. Which was easy—they were distinct impressions.

He paused, listening for me.

I paused, holding my breath, giving him nothing to hear.

Then, when I was a few feet behind him, I said, "*Hey!*"

He swung toward me.

Had I been him, I would have shot as I swung around. Like I said, immediate response is what keeps you alive in combat.

But he didn't shoot as he swung round, and as soon as he faced me, I jammed the half-a-ski-pole's spike into the hollow of his throat, while my other hand slapped that little .25 out of his hand, where it dropped like a doe turd in the snow.

His mouth was open wide. Gurgling. His eyes were open wider. Bulging. He was tottering. The half a ski pole was sticking out of his neck like an Indian had flung a spear at him, pissed off about the land grab.

The hill was steep enough to encourage him toppling forward, and the damnedest thing happened: apparently when that spike hit his spine, it couldn't break through to the other side, so for a few moments that wooden half-a-pole supported him. He wasn't quite dead yet, and his hands were waving like a skier trying to keep his balance.

Then the wood snapped and he was face down. Red bled down into the white-topped earth like a ghastly cherry snow-cone.

I didn't bother retrieving the .25. He was dead, all right. Funny thing was, before long the Outfit clean-up crew would come and collect the seminar participants and perform other housekeeping duties, with no idea another corpse was just up the hill from them. Sorry, up the mountain.

And Dan's death would provide a crime scene that would really have the local sheriff's department wondering.

For years.

Before I left him there, I got in his pocket for his Jaguar keys. Then I headed down the hill in the moonlight, winding through the trees, taking my time, breathing easy, beat but exhilarated. Not getting killed can do that.

I had to start up the Jag and ease it forward, before I could get out and retrieve my nine millimeter from where it had been out of reach. Which I did, and tucked the Browning back in my jacket pocket.

Then I got in the Jag and drove off. Driving away from the Lake Geneva Golf and Ski resort, I passed a black van marked Acme Cleaning Services. Maybe it was the Chicago clean-up crew, maybe not.

Still, it made me smile. Made me think of the Road Runner.

But I didn't hit my horn and go "beep beep."

# FIFTEEN

Dawn was taking its own sweet time coming, and right now all I wanted to do was to beat it home. I had just somehow made it through one of the longest nights of my life, and come out the other side alive, and now I could trade the cold for a warm bed. I hoped I'd be sharing it with Lu, unless she'd finally decided enough was enough and headed back to St. Paul.

But she hadn't, because the Camaro was still parked on the gravel apron in front of the A-frame, next to my Firebird, which she'd driven back here. That got a smile out of me. Lu still here, and that warm bed waited. What more could a man want?

I went up the short flight of steps to the deck and peeked in between where the drapes didn't quite meet at the sliding doors. Unless they'd been drawn really tight, I should be able to get a glimpse in at the living room.

And there she was, seated on one of the ottomans of the sectional couch by the conical metal fireplace, which she had going. She was in a light blue silk robe, looking at the flames, their reflection dancing on the slick cloth of the garment. Her blonde hair touched her shoulders, looking full and well-brushed; she must have showered when she got back.

Couldn't blame her. Even a tough cookie like Lu might want to wash away the memory of the bodies we found at the chalet, and ease the stresses and forget the dangers of the last few days.

She'd left the sliding door unlocked for me, which wasn't smart, but what the hell. Anyway, I wasn't dumb enough not to have the nine millimeter in hand when I slipped through the drapes into my living room, my eyes on her, but the alarm in those Asian orbs of hers, when she swung that unusual beautiful face toward me as I entered, hadn't come soon enough to help.

The barrel of an automatic was already against my right temple, right against it, and a male hand was plucking my nine mil from my fingers, a kid getting a toy gun taken away by a parent who didn't approve of such violent playthings.

I hadn't even seen him yet, tucked back there against the drapes to my right, waiting. The voice, belonging to Henry Poole, said, "Welcome home…*Quarry*, isn't it?"

I'd assumed he'd be in the wind. The only cars I'd seen in the front and rear lot of Wilma's had been employees' ones. No unfamiliar car parked along my lane and certainly not in front of the A-frame with the Camaro and Firebird. So I'd dismissed it. Stupidly.

"Hello, Hank," I said. "That's what you said to call you, right?"

"You bet. Hands behind your head now. Lock your fingers."

I did that and he patted me down one-handed and found no other weapons on me. I didn't have any to find. While he did that, my eyes went to Lu, her expression barely changed yet managing to convey a wealth of apology. Pros like us shouldn't be taken down so easily. But then we shouldn't have just had the night we'd shared.

"Okay," he said. "Have a seat."

I moved slowly over to the sectional couch, but not near where Lu sat on her ottoman; I glanced back at Poole who had my nine mil in his left hand and a Colt Combat Commander .45 in his right hand, its snout bearing a big and almost otherworldly noise suppressor—this was almost certainly the gun that had snuffed out those three seminar participants.

Though he was behind me, walking me over, I had not been

specifically directed where to sit. I wanted to be as far away from Lu as possible without my buddy Hank objecting—if he was going to shoot us, make him do it one at a time, so *somebody* besides this fucker Poole had a chance of surviving.

I settled on the same section of the sofa as when I faced Lu's late partner, Bruce Simmons, whose place opposite me Poole eased into, keeping that gun trained. He was in a sharp dark suit and pale yellow shirt, no tie, typical of the dress back at the Cayman Islands chalet get-together. My nine mil was stuffed in his waistband. The only light in the big A-ceilinged room came from that fireplace.

The once-handsome man, who'd fought advancing years with plastic surgery, again brought to mind the Phantom of the Opera in the orange and blue flickering flames thrown by the fireplace. Funny. This was my second fireside chat in the space of a few hours with somebody who wanted me dead.

Or did he?

*Why the hell was I still alive?*

I am, if nothing else, a dangerous motherfucker who will kill you without blinking if you pose a threat. Nothing personal, mind you. But particularly if you are somebody like this burn-victim-looking bastard, who has his own killing ways, you will get the switch thrown on your life by me with none of the fanfare of an electrocution by the state.

*And he had to know that.*

That slit on his face was forming something that was supposed to be a smile. "Wondering why you're still alive?"

I said nothing. Did nothing. But he was a perceptive son of a bitch, wasn't he?

*And why did he know to call me Quarry?*

"You must have so many questions," he said. "Would you like to pose them? I might miss something, if I just start rattling on."

Again I glanced at Lu at her fireplace perch. Her eyes widened and she shrugged, just barely, obviously not caring to make any sudden move that might get her shot—or me, either, for that matter.

When I'd glimpsed her from outside through where the drapes didn't quite meet, she had been turned toward the fire, her profile on display. Now she had slowly swung around so that she could watch the confrontation between me and my guest.

Just sitting there, hands folded in her lap, the half nearer the fire alive with fluctuating flame, the other half in shadow. I'm sure she was as confused as I was about still being alive.

As for Poole, he was no dummy. Where he sat, with his big ray-gun rod pointed at me, he was back away from me far enough that I couldn't kick the thing out of his hand. And if I jumped him, he could take me down like a skilled hunter does a duck on the fly. Better than that, actually—no distance involved.

Unless I really caught him off-balance.

"Mr. Quarry? Do you have questions, or do you prefer a soliloquy?"

Like *To be or not to be*? With this guy choosing the second option? I almost asked as much, but smart-ass remarks to guys holding guns on you, particularly individuals who have been indulging in wholesale murder lately, well…that made for less than stellar strategy.

I said, "I do have a few questions."

He nodded a little, a gracious mini-bow. "Please."

"That was you back there. At the chalet."

His eyebrows rose as far as the stretched skin would allow. "Doing the killing? Of course."

"And at the Vanhorn place? Him and the two watchdogs?"

"Yes."

"Do you have any other hobbies?" Okay, I couldn't help myself. Once a smart-ass, always a smart-ass.

And maybe it wasn't even a bad strategy at that, because it made him chuckle. Not laugh. Chuckle.

"I do, actually," he said. "I'm a collector of sorts."

"Not stamps, I'm guessing. Old records maybe? Comic books? Or…how about money?"

He nodded. He seemed loose-limbed, but that gun of mine in his paw stayed steady. "You are a good judge of character, Quarry. Money is my passion, all right. But you are reckless. No. *Audacious.* What else would you call this business of yours you've made a go of, for…what? A decade, or nearly so?"

So he knew.

Still, I had to ask: "What business is that?"

He shrugged. "Frankly, I don't know exactly. Neither did my friend, Vanhorn."

"Your friend?"

He nodded. "We weren't partners, but unlike the other agents …you call us 'brokers,' I believe, because you were once the favorite of that pretentious twit out of the Quad Cities—the Broker? Right?"

No reason denying it. And Broker *had* been pretentious.

So I nodded.

"Anyway," Poole said, looking like Joan Crawford in a horror movie in her later years when they were taping her skin back, "the agents, the brokers, the Envoy? They didn't work together. They barely knew each other. But Charles Vanhorn and I got well acquainted, were put in touch by certain Chicago individuals, and would from time to time help each other out. For various reasons, having to do with personnel and sometimes location, I would take on a job for him and he for me."

Why the hell was he telling me this?

But I said, "I can see how that might come in handy."

His shoulders went up and down, but again that didn't cause the gun-in-hand to lose its steadiness.

"It did," he said. "And we were friendly. After all, we were in the same line, but a line that we couldn't discuss with just anyone. We both had straight ventures going—successful ones, not just covers—and, well, you don't go to the Rotary Club and talk over your business woes or even successes, when they have to do with *our* kind of contracts."

"I can see that."

The Asian eyes over by the fireplace widened. *Was this guy nuts?* she seemed to be asking. I flicked her the barest look that said, *Who the hell knows?*

"So," he said, "Charles and I would discuss just what it was we thought was going on, where these periodic disrupted jobs and fallen pros were concerned. The deaths of our hired assassins often seemed accidental. The same was true of the individuals who'd taken out the contracts—occasionally one would die, again under mysterious circumstances. And it was sporadic enough…once or twice a year, out of any number of contracts …that it took time for our suspicion to grow into something more."

I knew what this was about now, of course. I'd known for a while. I knew why I wasn't dead, just another corpse with my blood and brains soaking a carpet or my pillow.

Yet.

I asked, "What did you and your friend Charles come up with?"

His gun-in-hand gestured, just a touch. "Well, as you may have gathered, we *did* know the Broker. Both Charles and I. In the early days, the regional set-up that since developed was in its earliest stages. So we knew about him. We'd even heard about you. You were something of a star in this business, Quarry."

Who doesn't like a compliment?

I said, "Not a good business to stand out in, actually."

The capped teeth flashed in a smile. "True. And when the Broker was killed, you weren't immediately suspected. Why, that would have been like patricide, wouldn't it? You being his favorite and all. But then, you dropped out of sight. Dropped out of the business. Which was right around when those contracts and clients and killers of ours started going…what's a good way to put it?"

"Tits up?"

Poole laughed. Jesus, all this guy needed was a pipe organ and a cackle to go flat-out Phantom.

He said, "That's as good a way as any. So we deduced you must have laid hands on the Broker's, what, special address book? And, now and then, followed one of our people to the job at hand, ascertained and approached the intended target, and offered help…for a price? That more or less it?"

"More or less." Exactly fucking it.

That smile was meant to be pleasant, I thought. Hard to tell. "Other questions, Quarry?"

"Were you really drunk back at the chalet?"

The change of subject stopped him, but for just a second. "Oh, no. Of course not."

"So that was staged? To get your girlfriend and those other women out of there, before…?"

Before the carnage began.

"Sort of," he said off-handedly, again gesturing just a tad with the gun-in-hand. "Two people in each murder room, that would have been a lot to deal with. So much more could go wrong." He shuddered. "Couldn't have any silly women running around the place screaming. Anyway, killing them wouldn't accomplish anything that simply sending them away from there wouldn't. Six people dead, including three beautiful women? What a media circus *that* would create! And, anyway, please—I'm no monster."

*Oh-kay.*

I asked, "So then your Playmate was in on it?"

"Oh, hell no! You have a satellite dish, don't you? I saw it outside, of course. Big unsightly things, but they do open up the world, don't they?"

"Afraid you lost me there."

"Well, I only meant you probably have access to the Playboy Channel. And my girlfriend, as you quaintly put it, has appeared in several original movies of theirs." He seemed a little proud of that, yet he added, "If you've seen her act, you'll know I couldn't risk giving her a speaking part."

"So when you slapped her around and shook her like a rag doll, it was for her own good."

"It was. And I will make it up to her. She'll understand. She'll come around." He shrugged. "She likes the finer things."

Finer things including *this* prick? And it seemed to me he was at least as pretentious as the Broker.

I said, "This is about the list, isn't it?"

That gash on his face did its pseudo-smile. "Knew it wouldn't take you long, my friend."

I was his friend now.

I asked, "Didn't you get Vanhorn's list from his wall safe? I'd guess his list and the Broker's were much the same."

"That may well be the case. But I did not find it when I... called on Charles recently, and its whereabouts are unknown. Perhaps the local police got it, and have no idea what they have."

"So you want the Broker's list," I said. "Understood. But it's old. Almost ten years, Hank. Can't guarantee every address."

"I have my eyes open."

He sure did. I didn't see how he ever got them closed.

I said, "I assume you view those names, and the information that goes with them, as assets. Which makes this part of your expansion. Your takeover of the entire region, which included removing your competition a few hours ago."

He nodded. No attempt at a smile now. The gun wasn't smiling either.

"So you want me to give it up," I said. "The Broker's list. I get that."

That was why I was still breathing. Temporarily. Lu, too. She'd have been dead already, but likely he figured her continued existence might serve as an inducement for me to cooperate.

"I want the list," he said, with a single nod. "The names, the information. But I'm not unreasonable. I don't expect something for nothing."

"In other words," I said, "you'll let me live."

"Yes."

Well, that was great to hear! Why wouldn't I trust *this* fuckhole?

"But there's more," he said, like an infomercial pitchman getting ready to throw in an extra Vegematic. "You can work for me, if you're interested. Your skills are, well, well-known if not quite legendary. You'll get the best paying contracts. Work as little or as much as you like."

"I sort of retired from that," I said. "I've kind of been working the other side of the street."

He nodded. Still reasonable. "All right. Understood. But what if we were to become partners?"

Like he'd been with his friend, the late Charles Vanhorn?

"What did you have in mind?" I asked, letting it play out.

"A twenty percent kickback on any income the names on that list generate."

I grinned. "How about twenty percent of your overall take, as the *über*-Broker?"

He frowned a little. "No. You wouldn't deserve that, would you?"

Hell, the one thing I hoped I'd never get was what I deserved.

I said, "How about ten percent of everything? Nothing extra for the list income."

He shook his head. "No. I think my offer is fair. And it's firm."

All right, now—this guy really was no dope. No stooge. He obviously had no intention of giving me anything but a bullet. But by negotiating like this, he clearly figured he'd make me believe his offer was the real thing. Unfortunately for him, I was no dope or stooge, either.

Still, he was the guy with the gun. Always a plus in any negotiation.

I took some air in. "Twenty percent on the Broker-linked income," I said, nodding. "It's a deal."

No handshake followed.

But he did give me his biggest smile yet. It was like a wound opening back up. "Good! Good. Let's start with the list itself. Turn it over and I'll leave you and your charming friend to enjoy the coming day. Dawn is on the way."

"What if I don't keep the list here? What if it's in a safe deposit box, or buried in a friend's back yard?"

He only smiled a little. "If the latter, we'll find a shovel. If the former, we'll go there together when the bank opens. A local bank, is it?"

"It's not in a local bank. Not in any bank." I pretended to mull it. "It's here, Hank."

He straightened a little. "Excellent. Why don't you get up slowly and lead me to wherever it is you keep it."

I gestured, a small one, at my nine mil in his hand. "Why don't you put your gun away first?"

"Afraid I can't do that. We haven't built up that level of trust as yet."

I wondered what level of trust he'd built with his old pal, the Envoy.

"I get that," I said, "but I'm unarmed."

"You may have a gun tucked away with the list, or lead me to where a gun is waiting with no list at all, hmm?"

I shook my head. "There's no hidden gun, Hank. And we're friends now, right? Business partners. I have the list, it's right here nearby, and it isn't under the floorboards in a box with a gun in it or a rattlesnake waiting or anything. But I don't care to have an automatic in my face. Makes me nervous."

He nodded and lowered the gun and I jumped him.

Took him off to the side of the couch section where he'd been sitting and tumbled onto the floor, about where Simmons had died. We rolled, ending up with him on top as I tried to wrest the gun from his grasp till he freed up one hand to yank my nine mil from his waistband and shoved the gun in me, right in my belly.

He got to his feet and pointed both guns down at me. "Stay there!" he said, looking flummoxed.

While I hadn't accomplished much other than to surprise and rattle him, without any hidden snake's help, he was glaring down with a grimace on that tight terrible mask of a face, likely wondering if he shouldn't just go ahead and kill me and then rip the place apart till he found what he was after.

He stood there breathing hard, trying to decide, maybe thinking that shooting me in various non-lethal areas might make me talk. The scuffling put Lu, on her perch behind us, out of his view, and she got up, quick and quiet, and slipped over to a nearby section of the couch and dug her hand down between cushions.

Must have been a habit of hers—squirreling her little collection of firearms around a room, in case she might need one, as she had back at our room at the chalet. Then she disappeared from my sight as she slipped around in back of him.

He didn't notice. He was too busy glowering down at me, saying, "You get me that fucking list now, or that slut of yours dies."

So much for his fine, friendly talk.

"You have a bad attitude," I advised him, "about women."

That must have alerted him enough to look over at Lu by the fireplace, only she wasn't there anymore, and he swung around and saw her in her new position, to the right near the draped sliding doors, and he was aiming both his ray-gun and my nine mil at her when, still prone, I kicked him in the ass with the flat of my right shoe, which had my right foot in it at the time, and he went stumbling toward her, till she greeted him with a bullet in the guts.

He stopped.

Sort of tottered and shimmied there for a few moments, his hands turning into fingers and the guns dropping, thankfully not firing when they hit, *clunk clunk*, and then she gave him two more in the belly to think about. He crawled on the floor, trying to get to those doors, leaving a snail-like trail, only not slimy silver but a brilliant red, then he just lay there on his side, legs up fetally, whimpering, his hands clutching his shredded skin over the punctured intestines within, blood oozing between fingers like water from a squeezed sponge.

Some of that blood had jumped out of him and onto her nice

blue robe. She removed the garment, tossing it with a disgusted cringe. All she wore beneath were the orange bikini undies I'd seen before.

She gathered the guns and set her small one and Poole's big clunky thing on the kitchenette counter, then brought along my nine mil as she headed back over to me. I was still down on the shag carpeting, on my ass, breathing hard.

"Thanks," I said.

We could hear him whimpering.

I said, "No head shot?"

She half-smiled. "And risk you getting your boyish face splashed again? No, gut-shot will do the trick nicely. He's an evil bastard and he deserves some suffering before the lights go out."

"Agreed." I was just starting to push up when she spoke.

"Now," she said. She loomed over me and I thought she was going to hand me the automatic, but instead she pointed it at me and said, "About that list...."

## SIXTEEN

"Really?" I said.

Lu and my own gun looked down at me. Her tanned legs seemed endless. Her breasts threw a voluptuous shadow on my fallen self.

"I don't want to kill you," she said. "Please don't make me kill you."

"No intention of doing that," I said, on my back but with my hands up in surrender.

Seemed to me she was having to try too hard to keep her tone businesslike; something emotional was trying to show through that she couldn't quite beat back, and I would swear her eyes were moist.

"I just want the list," she said. "I just want the Broker's file of names, addresses and information. Means nothing to you. You can't use it anymore. What you've been up to these past ten years has been exposed. And you have no desire to use it the way the Broker or Envoy did, right? So let's make it easy. Just hand it over and I'll get out of your life. No harm, no foul."

I was sitting up now.

I shrugged. Said, "Okay. You're right. I have no desire to be a goddamn booking agent for professional killers. But as far as being exposed? Everybody who knows about me is dead—Simmons, Vanhorn and friend Poole, over there…I think he's dead now, anyway. Not making noise anymore."

The wide mouth twisted in a small but distinct sneer. "I wish it had taken him longer."

"Me, too. And the only *other* person who knows what I've been up to, Lu, is you."

Her eyes bore in on me. "Would you kill me?"

I gazed right back at her. "Would you kill me?"

The gun lowered just a hair and she sighed and I hooked my foot under her ankle, and rolled to the left and took her down. She didn't land very hard, but the surprise of it made her grip loosen and I was right there to snatch the nine mil out of her fingers.

Then it was me standing, looming, and she was looking up in a pile, the Asian eyes now as wide as they were beautiful, dark blue with gold flecks, like Swiss schnapps.

She swallowed, head lowered but eyes aimed up, and said, "I wouldn't have killed you, Jack. I really wouldn't have."

"I'd like to think that."

She was shaking her head, just a little. "But if you intend to keep using that list…can you really afford to have me out there somewhere, knowing what I know? Particularly if I go back to taking contracts?"

I frowned at her. "Do you *want* me to kill you?"

"Not particularly." Her chin came up. "Let's talk about it. Like civilized people. See if we can come to some reasonable… understanding. Doesn't have to be like this."

"You started it," I reminded her, one child to another.

The wide mouth worked up a smile. "Let's call it our first lovers' quarrel.…Why don't you let me sit down somewhere that isn't the floor?"

I shook my head. "I have no way to know how many little pop guns you've spirited around the room, under this pillow and between what cushions. No. *I'll* sit down."

I did so, on a sectional piece that was close enough to her down there to maintain control of her, but not so close as to risk her making a move on me.

She did sit up, though, and hugged her legs to herself. There was something youthful about it. Which was maybe calculated.

"So we talk," I said.

"You first," she said.

I took air in and let air out. "All right. I think I instinctively knew, despite my liking for you, never to allow myself to get close to you again. That's why ten years passed before we reconnected…and it took you being the instigator." I nodded back at the dead man. "You and Poole set this whole thing in motion, didn't you?"

"What?"

"How you two got together, I don't know. But he and your late Envoy were tight, so that's probably part of it. You were the one who put the pieces together about what I'd been up to—you were there, ten years ago, on my first time using the list. Your partner on that job went down, and the client who took out the contract also met an unfortunate end. That got you thinking from the very start."

"Did it?"

"You knew all along that I was the target on your latest job. You played me like a cheap kazoo, didn't you? You would save me, killing your partner Simmons, and draw me into attending that seminar. When we went to Wilmette, to beard the Envoy in his den, you'd already killed him and his two security guards. You or Poole had. Meanwhile, you *helped* me. Fucked me, in several senses, and knew damn well that Poole would get rid of his rival brokers at the chalet and then I would be set up for the fall. But it didn't quite work out that way, did it?"

She covered her face with a hand. Emotion finally breaking loose. Couldn't blame her. I had some of that showing in my voice, too, with nothing I could do about it, because I had come to care for this woman. Or anyway for the woman she pretended to be.

"And finally, just now," I said, "you get rid of Poole. Leaving you in a position to take over the Midwest as the most beautiful businesswoman who ever ran a Murder, Incorporated set-up. Maybe the first. Now all you have to do is get the list out of me, and then—of course—tie off the one last loose end that I've become."

She lowered her hand from those striking features, which I'd figured would be streaked with tears. But she was smiling. Wide and big, and laughing too. Her eyes *were* tearing up. I had got that much right, sort of.

"Jack! Do you really *believe* that shit? If you weren't dead-on-your-feet tired, would you even come up with such over-complicated drivel?"

She stood.

Still seated, I trained the nine mil on her. "What are you doing? Sit the hell back down!"

But she didn't listen. She came over, a beautiful woman, so tall and tanned in the bright orange bikini undies, and she put a hand on my shoulder like she was bestowing a blessing, as if oblivious to the Browning automatic I still pointed at her, its nose just inches from her supple flesh.

"Here is the one thing," she said, gesturing with an upraised forefinger, "that I held back from you. I was suspicious of Simmons and Vanhorn—I could tell they were up to something. And when I got here, to your little pine-cone-covered corner of the world, and discovered you were the target? I wasn't sure I wanted to be part of it. That first night, I was standing—" She bobbed her head toward the front of the room and the sliding doors. "—just out there, on your deck, listening. I heard everything Bruce told you, about how he and the Envoy had figured out what you've been up to these past ten years, and the business proposition he made to you, if you would just hand over the list. Then you two got into it, with it looking like he might cap you, and those sliding doors were open...and I made my choice. I saved your ass, lover, and killed my longtime partner for you. I didn't like him much, anyway."

I narrowed my eyes at her. "You expect me to buy that the rest of it...from the trip to Wilmette on through the seminar stay...."

She shrugged. "Was all legit. I was just your trusty sidekick. Tonto and the Lone Ranger, only with bedroom privileges. No more, no less."

She moved away from me, in her bare feet, and returned to that ottoman by the fire, which was still going, maybe not as strong, but snapping and crackling and popping, just like Rice Krispies when the milk hits. She perched there, on a piece of furniture where there'd been no way for her to conceal one of her little .25s or .22s, and I came over and sat opposite her.

Her hands were on her knees, rather primly, but part of that was to show she wasn't playing any tricks.

"I apologize," she said.

"What for?" I asked. Still training the automatic on her, but not so...intensely.

She made an embarrassed face. "Holding you at gunpoint. Wasn't right. I should have had more faith in you."

"Should you?"

She nodded. "Look. We shared some lovely pipe dreams about going off together, you maybe joining me in St. Paul, me maybe even staying here with you, or possibly something completely different, like the Pythons say. Something new. After all, who besides you and me could understand the life we've been leading for so long? We wouldn't have to keep anything from each other. No apologies. It's nice, to think of that."

"Is it?"

"You *know* it is, Jack. But here's the thing. Here's why I thought it would take a gun to make you listen. To cooperate. *I do want that list.* I want out of the killing game, sure, but in a way it's all I know. My antiques business, much as I love it, is just a front. A money laundry. I don't have much put away, really. I live fairly high on the hog, you might say. I like nice things. Sue me."

"Your point being?"

"My point being, I *do* want to be a new broker in this business. Getting older makes field work hard. And riskier—how many scrapes have I narrowly slipped out of, over the years? Recently, especially? But if I spend ten years or so booking such gigs, let's call it, I could amass some real savings. Could retire to that life of leisure you hear so much about."

"That's your dream, Lu? Becoming regional murder sales manager?"

"No. My dream is actually smaller, Jack. I don't have the contacts that Bruce did, through the Envoy, to put a team of pros together. So your list…the names that don't belong to those you've dispatched, anyway…would be my assets starting out. And I'd gather more talent, likely through the Outfit, who if they see I'm doing a good job, would hand me some of the business those seminar attendees used to handle. Somebody would have to cover that, after all. So. I guess I'm no better than Bruce or Poole. I want the list to use it. To make money from it."

I tossed the gun on the couch next to me. "You should have just asked."

"Huh?"

"I don't want or need the fucking thing. It's all yours."

She was goggling at me. "You're serious."

"I am too tired to be anything but. It *is* in a safe deposit box, though. We'll have to go get it, later today. After we catch some sleep, okay?"

"You really *are* serious."

"As a heart attack. I have one demand, though. Well, request."

She frowned. "So there *is* a catch?"

"There's a catch. You need to help me get rid of this latest body."

She started to laugh and then we were hugging and smiling.

Don't you just love a happy ending?

Dawn finally arrived, the horizon over the lake as orange as Lu's undies, turning the few clouds in the deep blue sky the same near-fire color, which was also shimmering on the ebony water. The beauty of it only lasted a few moments, but so many good things are fleeting.

I headed out in the Jag with Lu following in the Camaro. We left the sports car along the side of a back road, with Poole jammed in its trunk, a bullet hole pocking the driver's side door. Another mystery for the county sheriff not to unravel, or for the Chicago boys to cover up.

That was when I shoved Lu into the front seat and said, "Good riddance, bitch," and shot her.

Of course I didn't.

Jesus, I'm not a monster, either.

What she and I did was spend much of the day in bed, mostly sleeping but also forgiving each other for that sad awkward scene this morning by frantically humping…but only after we'd caught some Z's.

I had an arm around her, on my back with my head against a pillow, her snuggling close.

"I have three grand," she said, "that was my share of the down payment for killing you, Quarry."

"God, how much was the overall contract?"

"Twelve g's."

Dan Clark had said I rated.

She said, "I feel weird about that money."

"What do you mean?"

"You know. How to *spend* it. Kind of blood money, isn't it? I mean, we don't kill friends, right?"

I shrugged. "Money doesn't know where it comes from. Of course, I put a real effort in, these past few days, and all *I* got out of it was not getting killed."

Her hand slipped under the covers and found what she was looking for. "*That's* all you got out of it?"

"Maybe not all."

"I have an idea."

I was getting one myself, but I said, "Yeah?"

"Twenty-five hundred would go a long way toward a little getaway. Bunch of places in the Caribbean don't require a passport. We can just hop a plane at O'Hare. Sun and fun and food and fucking and we can gamble a little. Some incredible casinos. You'd love it."

I smiled and considered that. "Take a vacation on the money you got paid for killing Quarry? Yeah. That sounds about perfect. As long as it isn't the Cayman Islands."

So Lu got the list, and I got her sweet companionship in St. Croix, a fair trade if there ever was one. I could write it up for you, but there's no violence at all. Just a bunch of sex.

And you're better than that.

## AUTHOR'S NOTE

Despite its period setting, *Killing Quarry* is not exactly an historical novel, and does not intend to suggest actual people or events, other than passing references to newsmakers and celebrities.

While the Lake Geneva Playboy Club Hotel, which opened in 1968 and was hugely successful for years, did close down in the early 1980s, it was not re-opened by Chicago-based organized crime interests—my suggestion of that in this novel is, like the rest of it, wholly fictional. Also, the geography of the actual facility is not strictly as it is depicted here. Much remodeled and updated, the former Playboy Club Hotel re-opened in 1994 as the Grand Geneva Resort and Spa, a highly regarded AAA Four-Diamond resort.

Information about the Cayman Islands and their banking system was culled from a number of Internet sources, as were any other number of topics from popular music to fashion, from automobiles to Solo cups. I lived through the 1970s and '80s, but based upon how frequently I have to research just about everything about those years, I was definitely not paying attention.

As readers who have followed the Quarry novels know, the narratives fall into several categories, the two major ones being Quarry's time as a hitman and Quarry's years hiring out his services to the targets of other hitmen. This novel is the last, chronologically, of the second group of novels; this is not to say other "list" narratives may not yet appear. Since returning to the character in *The Last Quarry* (2006), I have been jumping around in the continuity—the original four books were written in the '70s with another in 1987—staying (usually) in a '70s/'80s time frame, filling in the blanks as they occur to me.

Thus a series that began as contemporary has, like its author, become a period piece.

This novel is specifically a sequel to *Quarry's Deal* (originally titled *The Dealer*), first published in 1976. That novel, with an afterword by me, is available in a new edition from Hard Case Crime. By the way, I never anticipated writing a sequel to a novel I wrote 43 years ago.

My thanks to HCC editor Charles Ardai for his continued good will and support; my friend and agent Dominick Abel; and of course my wife, writer Barbara Collins, my first reader/editor, who provided vital input during the writing of this novel.

# WANT MORE QUARRY?

*Try These Other Quarry Novels From*
MAX ALLAN COLLINS *and*
HARD CASE CRIME...

## The First Quarry

The ruthless hitman's first assignment: kill a philandering professor who has run afoul of some very dangerous men.

## Quarry in the Middle

When two rival casino owners covet the same territory, guess who gets caught in the crossfire…

## The Last Quarry

Retired killer Quarry gets talked into one last contract—but why would anyone want a beautiful librarian dead…?

## Quarry's Ex

An easy job: protect the director of a low-budget movie. Until the director's wife turns out to be a woman out of Quarry's past.

## The Wrong Quarry

Quarry zeroes in on the grieving family of a missing cheerleader. Does the hitman's hitman have the wrong quarry in his sights?

*Or Read On for Sample Chapters From*
*The Book Where We First Meet Lu,*
QUARRY'S DEAL!

# ONE

I waited for her to come, and when she did, so did I. I asked her to lift and she lifted and let me get my hands out from under her. Here I'd been cupping that ass of hers, enjoying that fine ass of hers, and then we both came and suddenly her ass weighs a ton and all I can think about is getting my hands out from under before they get the fuck crushed.

I rolled off her.

"Was it good for you?" she asked.

"It was fine."

There was a moment of strained silence. She wanted me to ask, so I did: "How was it for you?"

"Fine," she said.

That taken care of, I got off the bed, slipped into my swim trunks, trudged into her kitchen, and got myself a bottle of Coke.

"Get some Kleenex for me," she called from the bedroom.

I was still in the kitchen. I said, "You want something to drink?"

"Please! Fix me a Seven and Seven, will you?"

Jesus, I thought. I put some Seagram's and Seven-Up and ice in a glass, got her some Kleenex from the bathroom, and went into the bedroom, where she took both from me, setting the glass on the nightstand, stuffing the Kleenex between her legs.

There was a balcony off the bedroom, through French doors, and I went out and looked down on the swimming pool below. It was mid-evening, and cool. Florida days are warm year round, they say, but the nights are on the chilly side, particularly a March one like this.

Not that the crowd of pleasure-seekers below seemed to mind.

Or notice. Lean tan young bodies, of either sex, their privates covered by a slash or two of cloth, basked in the flickering glow of the torch lamps surrounding the pool. Some of them lounged on towels and sun chairs as if the full moon, which I could see reflected in the shimmery green water of the pool, was going to add to their already berry-brown complexions. Others romped, running around the pool's edge or in the water splashing, perpetual twelve-year-olds seeking perpetual summer.

I watched one well-endowed young woman tire of playing water baby with a boyfriend, climb out of the pool, tugging casually at her flimsy top which had slipped down to reveal dark half-circles of nipple. She was laughing, tossing back a headful of wet dark blond hair, shoving at the brawny chest of the guy who was climbing out of the pool after her. He pretended to be overpowered by her nudge and waved his arms and made a show of falling back in, but she no longer seemed amused.

She wasn't beautiful, exactly. The girl in the bedroom behind me was more classically beautiful, with a perfect, high-cheekboned fashion model face and a slim but well-proportioned figure. A lot of the girls at this place (which was an apartment complex for so-called "swinging singles") were the model type; others were more All-American-style beauties, sunny-faced girls sung about in songs by the Beach Boys. She fit neither type.

Her face was rather long, her nose long and narrow, her eyes having an almost Oriental slant to them. Her mouth was wide and when she smiled, gums showed. Her figure was wrong, too: she was tall, at least an inch taller than my five ten, with much too lanky a frame for those huge breasts. Put that all together and she should have been a goddamn freak.

But she wasn't. The big breasts rode firm and high; she carried them well. Her face was unique-looking. You might say haunting. The eyes especially, which were dark blue with flecks of gold. Her voice was unusual, too—a rich baritone as deep as a man's, as deep as mine, in fact—but for some reason it only made her seem all the more feminine.

I didn't know her, but I knew who she was. I was here because of her. I'd been here, watching her, for almost a week now. If she noticed me, she gave no indication. Not that it mattered. The beard and mustache, once shaved off, would make me someone else; when we met in another context, one day soon, she'd have little chance of recognizing me, even if she had managed to pick me out of this crowd (which incidentally included several other beards and plenty of mustaches, despite the unspoken rule that tenants were to be on the clean-cut side in appearance, if not in behavior).

I hoped I wouldn't have to kill her. I probably would. But I hoped not. I wasn't crazy about killing a woman, only that wasn't the problem. I hadn't counted on her looking like this. Her picture had made her look almost homely. I'd had no idea she radiated this aura of some goddamn thing or another, some damn thing that made me want to know her, made me uncomfortable at the thought of having to kill her.

"Hey," she said.

I turned.

This one's name was Nancy. She was wearing a skimpy black bikini. She had short dark black hair and looked like a fashion model. Or did I mention that already?

"You want to go down and swim?" she asked.

"Later," I said.

"Is that Coke good?"

"It's fine."

"How come you don't drink anything but Coke and that? Got something against liquor?"

"No. I have a mixed drink sometimes."

"What d'you come out here for?"

"It's nice out here."

"Is it because you knew I'd smoke?"

"I guess."

"Don't you have a single fucking vice?"

"Not one."

"Tell me something."

"Okay."

"You always this blue after you do it?"

"Just sometimes."

"Every time. With me, anyway. You always get all, uh, what's a good word for it?"

"Quiet."

"No. Morose. That's the word I want."

"Quiet is what I get. Don't read anything into anything, Nancy."

"I knew a guy like you once. He always got…quiet… after doing it."

"Is that right."

"You know what he said once?"

"No."

"He said, 'Doing it is like Christmas: after all the presents are open, you can't remember what the fuss was all about.' " And she laughed, but it got caught in her throat.

"What are you depressed for?"

"I'm not depressed. Don't read anything into anything, Burt."

Burt is the name I was using here. I thought it sounded like a good swinging singles name.

"My husband used to get sad, sometimes, after we did it."

Him again. She talked about him all the time, her ex. About what a son of a bitch he was, mostly. He was an English professor at some eastern university, with rich parents who underwrote him. He (or rather they) paid for Nancy's apartment here in

Florida. There was a kid, too, a daughter I think, living with Nancy's parents in Michigan.

"You know what he used to say?" she asked.

"Something about Christmas?"

"No. He used to say that in France coming is called the little death."

"That's a little over my head, Nancy."

"Well, he was an intellectual. The lousy prick. But I think what it means is when you come, it's like dying for a second, you're going out of this life into some place different. You're not thinking about money or your problems or anything. All you can think of is coming. And you aren't thinking about that, either. You're just coming."

Down by the pool, the girl I'd come here to watch was sitting along the edge, kicking at the water, while her blond boyfriend tried to kid her out of her mood.

Nancy's hand was on my shoulder. I looked at her and she was lifting her mouth up to me, which meant I was supposed to kiss her, and I did. I put my hand between her legs and nudged her with a finger.

"Bang," I said.

She took my arm and pulled me into the bedroom.

# TWO

We went down for a swim afterwards. I let Nancy do the swimming. I like to swim, but I don't like crowds. You can't swim in a crowd. All you can do is wade around bumping into people. So Nancy swam and I watched.

I didn't watch Nancy, though. I just pretended to. What my eyes were really on was the young woman with the big breasts and Oriental eyes and muscle-bound boyfriend. The boyfriend had the look of a Hollywood glamour boy gone slightly to seed. Thinning hair; puffy face; on the road to a paunch.

She was bored with him. He'd given up trying to talk her out of her indifference to him and was sitting in a beach chair with a drink in his hands, watching a blonde in a yellow bikini who sat across the way looking as bored with her companion as the big-breasted Oriental-eyed girl was bored with him.

I was bored, too. I hadn't been here a week and I was suffocating. I live in Wisconsin, near the Lake Geneva vacation center, and the summer months around those parts are cherished and enjoyed and, in the freezing cold winter months, looked forward to. I'd come here expecting a similar attitude. Instead I found the year-round summer was not so much taken for granted as squandered. Made meaningless.

I never imagined yards of beautiful exposed flesh under sunny skies could get dull. I never thought cool evenings full of cool drinks and warm glances could grow monotonous. I never dreamed sex could become so tedious.

Nancy wanted it every time I turned around. Three or four times a day, and the first couple days I was glad to accommodate.

I'd gone for months without getting laid, and was more than ready. But after close to a week of it, I was just plain tired. The crazy part was what Nancy told me about the breakup of her marriage: "The son of a bitch was a sex maniac.... He didn't respect me as a person at all." She told me this while we were taking a shower together.

All of this was new to me. I had never had to maintain a relationship with one woman while watching another woman I would most likely have to kill. I was used to keeping those two particular compartments of my life separate. I led a relatively normal social life in Wisconsin, including an occasional Nancy. But the life away from home was something else again. The business part of my life, I mean. The killing.

Of course I was in a different business now; slightly different, anyway. A new, self-created business that would require an intermixing, now and then, of the social me and the other one.

And I was finding out now, in my first time out, that playing both roles at once could prove to be a little disturbing.

Or anyway, irritating.

Though considering the boredom of this would-be paradise, a touch of irritation was maybe a good thing. At least I was awake. Aware, always, I was here on business. Perhaps I should've been thankful I hadn't been seduced by the sex-and-sun, flesh-and-fun atmosphere of the place.

Only I was finding something else irritating. Or disturbing, anyway. I had developed a nagging fascination with the woman I was watching, that Oriental-eyed woman with the big breasts, a woman who didn't seem to quite fit in here, and that fascination was unhealthy as hell, especially since this was my first outing in my new (make that revised) line of work.

How much longer was I going to have to watch her? Another week? A month? Longer? I never have liked stakeout work, and this swinging singles lifestyle, with its fringe "benefit" of constant sex, seemed likely to kill me before I had a chance to kill anybody myself.

Maybe tonight would be different. After all, the afternoon had been different. The tall, busty woman I'd been watching these past few days had acted a little strange this afternoon. All week she'd been giddy, just another bubble-headed fun-seeker playing footsy and everything-elsey with her blond boyfriend. But this afternoon she'd gotten moody. Her face had taken on an almost grim look. Her efforts at having fun seemed just that: efforts. Efforts that had failed and lapsed into…what? Depression? No. More like seriousness. A serious mood, rather than a black or bitchy one.

Something was up, maybe.

Not me, certainly: I was wilted. Nancy was going to have to learn to respect me as a person—for the rest of the night, anyway.

Meanwhile the crowd in and around the pool was beginning to thin. Nancy begged off around two-thirty and by that time there was only half a dozen of us left. My dragon lady was one. Her blond hunk of manhood was another, only now he was in the water with a blond hunk of womanhood whose own hunk she had managed to lose, along with the top of her bikini, and two small but perfectly shaped boobs bobbled in the water like apples, pink apples, if there is such a thing, or even if there isn't. I didn't much care either way. I was too wrung out to care. Not so the two blonds: they climbed out of the pool giggling and one chased the other into the shadows.

That left me alone with her.

Which was not good. A harmless conversation, idly struck… and the ballgame was over. Of course there was a whole pool between us; better an ocean. I needed to stay just some anonymous bearded guy who she had never really looked at close, otherwise the entire deal was blown.

But she wasn't looking at me. She was looking at the water. Staring at it, the surface rippling with the slight breeze, the torch lights shimmering eerily in reflection.

And then she got up and went up the open stairway to the second level, where her apartment was.

I stayed behind. I was, to say the least, relieved. And now that I had the pool to myself, I could have a nice, private swim, which is a daily ritual of mine, whenever possible, anyway.

I dove in.

I'd just swum my sixth easy lap when she came down wearing a dark, mannish pants suit, suitcase in either hand, and headed into the parking lot, from which, moments later, came the sound of squealing tires.

# THREE

I could have followed her. I had my car keys in the pocket of my robe, which was with my towel, under the beach chair where I'd been sitting before I started my swim.

But I might have looked just a shade conspicuous jumping into the Opel GT soaking wet, in nothing but a pair of swim trunks, and considering I was already afraid she might have taken some notice of me, following her, at this moment, in my present condition, didn't seem, well, prudent.

The next best thing to following her was to find out where she was going.

So that's what I decided to do. Try to do, anyway.

I hadn't ever gotten in her apartment to look around, despite the number of days I'd been there. She hadn't left the grounds of the place since I'd arrived: she sent her boyfriend out to do the grocery shopping, and with all the drinking and sex available on the premises, who needed to go out for anything except supplies?

I maybe could have got in and searched her place while she was down by the pool with her blond plaything; she did spend a lot of time down there, after all. But who was to say when she or the plaything might tire of the pool and come up for a nap or something. And, too, during all but a few of the nocturnal hours, I was playing plaything myself, for Nancy, so when the fuck was I supposed to get in that apartment for a look?

Now.

Now I could do it. The dragon lady was gone, packed and left in the middle of the night, as a matter of fact, and her boyfriend was apparently shacked up, at least temporarily, with a new mistress…and I don't mean mistress in the modern sense, not exactly.

I mean mistress in the dictionary sense, "woman in authority, in control." Women ruled at that place. It should've been called the Amazon Arms (and not Beach Shore Apartments, which is redundant as hell, I know, but then the owner/manager's name was Bob Roberts, so you figure it). The Beach Shore rented exclusively to women. Divorced women, mostly, alimony-rich divorced women.

All the rooms had double beds, and there were a lot of men around, but the men would come and go, so to speak, and the women stayed on.

Which is why it hadn't been hard to infiltrate the place. I just dropped in one afternoon and sat by the pool, wearing my tight little trunks, and waited to be picked up. It wasn't as degrading as I'd imagined it, but it was degrading enough. As any woman reading this could tell you.

So now that the dragon lady was away, with an apparent rift developed between her and her plaything, I figured I'd find that apartment very empty. And the risk of being interrupted while I had my look around was little or no.

Getting in would be no problem. Getting in was never a problem around this place, in about any sense you can think of. The asshole who managed the place (the owner, old Bob Roberts, remember?) was never in his own apartment, as he considered that part of his function was servicing any of his tenants who were momentarily between playthings. He liked to tell his tenants his door was always open, and it was. So was his fly.

Anyway, I walked in one afternoon, found his master key in a drawer and took it to a Woolworth's in the nearby good-size town, where I had a dupe made, returned his key, and got back in bed with Nancy, all in the course of fifty minutes.

I used to be good at picking locks, but got out of the habit. For what I'd been doing the past few years, I'd seldom needed tools of that sort, as most of my work was in the Midwest, where security tends to be lax, where most doors can be opened with a credit card, and there are lots of other ways to get in a place if you have to, easier ways than picking a lock, I mean, which honest-to-Christ requires daily practice. Anybody tells you picking locks is easy is somebody who doesn't know how to pick locks.

I got out of the pool.

I put on my robe, went up the steps and inside, where I found the corridor empty and felt no apprehension at all as I worked the dupe of the owner/manager's master key in the lock and went in. I turned on the lights (the windows of her apartment faced the ocean-front side of the building, so no one was likely to see them on, and even so, so what?) and began poking around.

The apartment itself was identical in layout to Nancy's, except backwards, as this was on the opposite side of the hall. The decorating was very different, which surprised me: apparently each tenant could have her own decorating done, so where a wall in Nancy's had pastel blue wallpaper, light color blue like Wisconsin summer sky, the dragon lady had shiny metallic silver wallpaper; other walls were standard dark paneling in either apartment, but in this one, for example, a gleaming metal bookcase-cum-knickknack rack jutted across the living room, cutting it in half, with few books on it and a lot of weird African-looking statues and some abstract sculptures made of glazed black something. And where in Nancy's place there was a lot of wood, nothing furniture, everything antiques, this place had plastic furniture, metal furniture, glass furniture, all of it looking expensive and cheap at the same time.

In the bedroom, above the round waterbed, with its white

silk sheets and black furry spread, was a painting. A black square with an immense red dot all but engulfing it. Nancy had a picture above her bed, too. An art nouveau print of a beautiful woman in a flowing scarf against a pastel background. Nancy had an antique brass bed. I had the feeling these girls weren't two of a kind.

Meanwhile, I was going through things. The name she was using here was Glenna Cole, but I found identification cards of various sorts in several other names. The Broker's name for her was Ivy. Knowing Broker's so-called sense of humor, that probably came from poison ivy. Broker called me Quarry. Because (he said) a quarry is carved out of rock. The Broker's dead now.

I found a gun. A spare, probably. She wouldn't have taken her suitcases with her unless she was going off on a job. That was my guess, anyway, and it came from experience. Also, the gun was just a little purse thing, a pearl-handled .22 automatic, and I imagined she used something a little heavier than that in her work. A .38, at least. Speaking of which, I did find a box of .38 shells behind some lacy panties in a drawer, and that substantiated my guesswork, as there was no gun here that went with these shells.

What I didn't find was evidence of where she'd gone. I went through the wastebaskets, and I even went through a bag of garbage in her kitchen, and found nothing, no plane or bus reservation notice, no nothing. I even played the rubbing a pencil against the top blank sheet of a notepad trick, and while it seems to work on television, all I got for my trouble was dirty fingers.

I sat on an uncomfortable-looking comfortable couch in her living room and wondered what to do next.

That was when her boyfriend came in.